ON THE NIGHT SHE DIED

A Quarry Street Story

MEGAN HART

Blurb

Friendships. Love. Secrets.

Jennilynn Harrison left them all behind — her sister Alicia. Her friend-to-lover Ilya Stern. His younger brother Niko. The Stern brothers' step-sister Theresa.

Intertwined lives, all of them damaged by what happened on the night she died.

Copyright © 2018 by Megan Hart

All rights reserved.

No part of this book may be reproduced in any form or by any electronic or mechanical means, including information storage and retrieval systems, without written permission from the author, except for the use of brief quotations in a book review.

ISBN: **978-1-940078-54-0**

❦ Created with Vellum

Chapter 1
REBECCA

Now

Rebecca Segal hadn't been home in a long damned time, but if it was really the place where they *had* to take you in, she supposed a little gratitude on her part might not be out of line.

Yesterday, her mother's voice on the phone had been shaking, querulous, weak. She hadn't quite begged Rebecca to leave the sunny shores and warm waters of Cozumel, but the fact her mother might have felt as though she *had* to plead was more than enough to get Rebecca on the first flight home. She hadn't even packed her suitcase — there wasn't anything she owned that she couldn't afford to replace. She'd gone straight from the airport to the hospital.

Her father had died before she could get there.

Rebecca would regret that for the rest of her life. Not having the chance to say goodbye to her dad. Not being there as he drew his last breath. Not holding her mom's hand through his final moments. She could have blamed her mother for not calling her sooner, but the truth was, Rebecca had left home years ago and never returned no matter how many times her parents had asked, begged or pleaded, so if there was any blame to be laid, it was solely at Rebecca's own extravagantly shod feet.

"Hang on," she told the driver as they reached a stoplight. "Can you go by way of Zimmerman's diner?"

"It's called B's Diner, now. But sure, of course we can swing past," the guy said.

The driver looked old enough to remember when Zimmerman's had been in its heyday. For a moment, Rebecca considered asking him how long he'd lived in Quarrytown. Maybe they'd gone to school together. Maybe he was remembering her while she couldn't place a name to the face.

"How long has it had a new name?"

"About a year now. Do you want me to stop so you can run in?" The driver's eyes caught hers in the rearview mirror.

Rebecca shook her head and looked out the window. The building was the same as she remembered, but clearly updated. Paint, gleaming chrome, a new sign. She hadn't been inside a good old-fashioned diner in years. Screw gluten, lactose, sugar and fat-free. Greasy eggs and black bitter coffee sounded like heaven right about now.

"No, thanks," Rebecca said.

Quarrytown had seen a lot of other changes, not only a new diner. New strip malls filled in what had once been bare fields. Neighborhoods of identical houses lined up along gently curving streets with macadam so new it was still inky black. The old high school was still there, but an entire new wing had changed it drastically.

She closed her eyes and leaned back against the car's leather seat. She'd been surprised but grateful to find out she could call for a freelance driving service. The driver had told her, when she asked, that the service had only become available in Quarrytown a couple months before. It was nothing like the kind of black car treatment she was used to, but it was better than a cab. If she was going to stay in town for any length of time, she'd have to see about getting herself a permanent ride.

She could probably drive her dad's. The completely restored 1967 Chevy Impala had been his baby for the past four decades, and he'd been driving it right up until he got sick. The tears threatened then, but she fought them back fiercely. She hadn't broken down in the hospital, and she sure as hell wasn't going to do it in front of a stranger.

This car's tires rumbled, and Rebecca opened her eyes. The house on the hill hadn't changed. Gray paint with black trim, red front door still hung with the holiday wreath her mother insisted on every year, the way she always put a Christmas tree in the front room where the neighbors could see it, even though the Segals didn't celebrate the holiday. Rebecca craned her neck for a glimpse of that tree through the glass, but her driver was pulling up the driveway and around the back to the garage too fast for her to see anything but a glare of headlights.

Her mother had gone to stay with her sister Anne and hadn't been home in the past few days, so the back door opening, along with the spill of light onto the dark driveway, startled Rebecca. She leaned forward over the front seat to tap the driver on the shoulder. "Wait, please."

"Everything okay, Miss?"

Rebecca hadn't been a "miss" for about as long as she'd been gone from Quarrytown, but she didn't correct him. She was too busy studying the silhouette in the doorway. Mom had mentioned a daily caregiver for Dad, but there was no reason for him to be at the house now.

Besides, something in the figure's posture seemed familiar. She frowned, then let out a beleaguered sigh and rubbed at the tension spot between her eyes that she kept meaning to get taken care of with some fancy and expensive injections.

"It's fine," she said. "It's just my ex-husband. He's not supposed to be here."

"Do you need me to go in with you? Are you safe?"

Rebecca paused, surprised and a little touched at the offer. "Yeah, it's fine. I wasn't expecting him, that's all. I don't need you to go in with me. Thank you, though."

"I'm happy to walk up with you. Make sure it's all good." The driver had twisted around in the seat to look at her.

If he wasn't hitting on her right this minute, he'd definitely thought about it. She could see it in his eyes, a kind of assessing look that Rebecca had grown used to over the years. Even a few days ago, she'd probably have taken him up on the offer, if only because he was young, handsome, rough around the edges but trying hard, and it would have pissed off Richard to see her with another man, even one who she had no intentions of screwing. Well, maybe no *strong* intentions.

Right now, she was too tired for games like that. "I'm sure it's fine. Do you have a card? In case I need another…ride."

She let the words linger, suggestive, keeping eye contact a few seconds longer than necessary. The light in his gaze told her she'd been right about his attraction to her. Another time, Rebecca would have enjoyed it. Used it. Now, she'd turned her own stomach.

She took the card he offered and got out of the car. Richard was still in the doorway when she got to the back steps. She didn't say anything to him until she'd pushed past him and he closed the door behind her.

"I made a pot of coffee," Richard said. "Where's your mom?"

"She went to Aunt Anne's," Rebecca said. "How long have you been here?"

"An hour or so. I stopped over to see if you needed anything. I'm going over to my folks' house tonight. Don't worry," he added in a voice dripping with sarcasm, "I'm not sticking around."

Rebecca didn't need to ask him how he'd known where to find the spare key. Hell, Richard probably still had his own house key. Her parents had adored him, and unlike her, he'd never been a prodigal son. He'd been in this house more than she had in the past twenty years and definitely more often in the last ten since they'd gotten divorced.

"Have you talked to Grant?" Her question came out sounding too casual, with an undercurrent of strain. Her son hadn't answered her texts.

"I left a voicemail for him, but he hasn't called me back."

Rebecca took a grim gratification in knowing Grant wasn't giving his father any more response than he'd given her. It was a cold comfort, short-lived. She hadn't spoken, actually spoken, to her son in over a year. She'd given up calling when it became clear he was never going to return her messages. Texting, even without a reply, was easier. She sometimes stalked his social media, making sure he was all right. She sent him money that he never refused.

"I told him he could come and stay with me at my parents' house," Richard added.

Her lip curled a little bit at that, but she nodded without arguing about it. Grant was over twenty-one. An adult. He could make his own decisions. If that decision was his father and his paternal grandparents, so be it.

"It's cold," Rebecca said after a moment when she lifted the carafe from the coffeemaker.

"You know, you could just say 'thank you.'"

Carefully, Rebecca put down the carafe. She bit her tongue, a real, physical nip of it between her teeth. She held it there as she counted to ten, determined she wasn't going to lose her shit with him.

"My father died, Richie," she said finally in a dark, gritty voice that would have scared her, if she'd been on the receiving end of it. "How about you just…go."

Richard had never been scared of her. That might have been a huge part of the reason why their marriage failed. He'd never been able to see when he'd pushed her beyond the limits of her admittedly short temper. Or maybe he'd simply never cared. Right now, Rebecca was the one who didn't care. Not about saving her ex-husband's fragile feelings, not about being nice, and sure as hell not thanking him for doing something she hadn't asked him to do, something she neither needed nor wanted from him.

"I came here to see if you're all right —"

"Get out," she said through clenched jaws when he didn't move. "This is not your house. He was not your father."

Incredibly, Richard moved closer to her. His hand, heavy on her shoulder, caught in her hair where it had fallen out of the messy twist she'd been wearing since two days ago, when she'd been sunning herself on the beach in front of crystal blue waters and contemplating the night's entertainment in the form of a very cute pair of college boys on the activities staff who'd claimed to be working their way through school.

Rebecca shrugged away from his grip, giving his hand and then his face a long, disgusted look. "They're reading the will on Thursday. Isn't that what you really want to know?"

"That's not fair."

But it was true, she thought, watching his expression. If Richard had been close with her dad, it was because his own father had been Morris's best friend. They'd done business together. Gone on vacation. Golfed. Rebecca wouldn't go so far as to say her ex-husband wasn't sad about her father's death, but she wasn't going to pretend, the way he seemed to be, that he wasn't assuming that he'd been named in the will.

"Life's not fair," she shot back, instantly regretting how childish she sounded.

Richard had always brought out the worst in her, even during the times when it had been all right between them. She hadn't wanted to give him the satisfaction of knowing he'd gotten under her skin, but that would be giving him credit for having the ability to actually figure out the reasons for another person's emotional response beyond his own. She wasn't feeling charitable enough right now to go that far.

"Fine, I'll go. You have my number if you need me." Richard paused, maybe waiting for her to tell him that she needed him.

Rebecca hadn't needed him in a long time, and she wasn't about to start now. She waited until he'd gone out the back door, then locked it and slid the deadbolt shut after him. She wouldn't put it past him to try and come back.

In the fridge, she found an unopened bottle of Chardonnay, the good stuff. Her throat closed again as she thought about her dad cutting the wine with seltzer water for her mother, who'd always claimed she "didn't drink" but who could easily put away four or five "spritzers," when you got her going. Dad had favored heavy reds and smoky bourbon, but right now, an undiluted glass of white was going to have to do for his daughter. She'd raise a glass for dad in a few days, after she'd had time to go to the liquor store.

"God," she said aloud. "Save me from places where you can only buy booze from the state store."

Glass of wine in one hand, she headed for the stairs. She'd go to her old room. Take a long, hot bath. Tuck herself between clean, soft sheets. Sleep. In the morning she'd wake up and although her father wouldn't be there to greet her, at least she'd be here for Mom when she decided she was ready to come home from Aunt Anne's. Life would go on, not as they'd known it, but they would find a way to adjust.

Rebecca paused on the stairs to look at the array of framed pictures. Her smiling face, teeth glinting with metal braces. Another of her as a child, her hair in pigtails, her smocked dress a reminder of the horrors of past fashions. And there, in an oversized frame, her wedding photo.

She'd been pregnant with Grant in that picture, although at the time she'd been the only one who'd known. Even Richard hadn't known. She'd carried small. Hadn't even needed to let her dress out. Shaking her head at the disaster of her early nineties hair, the plethora of ruffles on the gown and its leg-o-mutton sleeves, Rebecca started to go back up the stairs. She paused again, looking at the photo.

She ought to have been happy on her wedding day, and she'd have said back then that she was. It was too easy to retrofit memories, to imagine she'd been cringing inside, that her wide smile had hidden fear and grief. Too easy, not what it had ended, to believe she'd known all along it was going to be a mistake. Looking at her younger self in the picture, Rebecca could remember being anxious but ready for her life to begin. She'd believed she was making the right choice when she married Richard.

With a low mutter, she tugged the picture off the wall. It left behind a fainter, paler mark against the mint green paint. Her wine sloshed in the glass. She tossed back the last of the drink and carried the picture in its frame down to the kitchen, where she set the glass on the counter and opened the back door. A few brisk steps took her to the wooden fence surrounding the tall garbage cans, and a yank opened the gate. The picture barely fit inside the biggest can, but when she shoved it, the glass broke along with the edges of the wood, and she was able to push the entire thing down deep into the can.

"There," she said aloud into the night. "Much better."

Chapter 2
JENNI

Then

It was October, but still so warm that the halter dress Jenni Harrison wore was almost too much for her to stand. When she swiped a tongue across her upper lip, she tasted salt. It reminded her of the summer and lazy days floating in the chilly waters of the quarry. Next summer would be the last one for her, she thought suddenly and with a frown. This was her last year of high school. A year from now, next October, if her parents had their way, she'd be firmly settled in some dorm, trying to figure out what she wanted to be when she grew up.

She didn't want to grow up.

But she didn't have to think about that now. Not tonight. Tonight she was going to be young and dumb and full of…she giggled to herself before she could finish the sentence. That was kind of gross, even if it did make her laugh. Her sister Alicia, two years younger, frowned.

Allie paced the floor of their shared bedroom, clearly

nervous, as she repeatedly tucked her straight, reddish hair behind her ears. "Did you get the beer?"

Of course she had. They were having the party across the street, at the Sterns' house. She hadn't had to work too hard to convince Ilya to host, but the party was all Jenni's idea, and you couldn't have a party without beer. Not a good one, anyway, and Jenni intended this party, this night, to be *epic*. Beyond anything anyone in this shitty little town had ever seen. If things went the way she'd planned, the dead end of Quarry Street would be on fire tonight — maybe even literally.

Maybe everything would burn.

Jenni laughed at her sister's anxious expression and tossed her hair over her shoulders. She'd been thinking of dying it. Black, maybe. Or streaks of color, kind of punk rock. Oooh, she could cut it short, maybe even shave it to the scalp…baby sister was staring, so Jenni pressed her lips together before saying, "Of course. I told you I would. A whole case."

"How did you get a whole case of beer?" Allie was still pacing. Her fingers clenched and curled, then released. She was clearly freaking out.

"Allie!" Jenni snapped her fingers in front of Alicia's face. "Chill. You're making me nervous."

"How did you get a case of beer?" Alicia lowered her voice to a hissing whisper.

Mom and Dad were still here, getting ready in their room down the hall. They were going away for the weekend, leaving Jenni in charge for the first time. At seventeen, she was supposed to be old enough to handle things. She should be proud they thought so, right? Allie clearly didn't think Jenni could handle shit, because she was still looking like someone had stuck her with a fistful of pins. For a second, Jenni wanted to put an arm around her younger sister and reassure her it would all be okay, and that if anything, she ought to be on her knees thanking Jenni for setting this up. Allie's cool factor was going to skyrocket after tonight.

It hadn't been that long ago that she and Allie had been "thick as thieves," as their mother said. Now Jenni couldn't remember the last time the two of them had really shared their secrets. And Jenni had plenty, didn't she? Allie probably didn't have a single one.

"I know a guy." Jenni shrugged again as she looked in the mirror to admire the heart-shaped pendant she knew Allie wanted, but which had been gifted to her. For a single moment she considered taking it from her neck and giving it to her sister, who certainly wanted it more than Jenni ever had.

Black flecks speckled the glass where the silvering had come off it in the back. This mirror was an antique, attached to an old dresser that had been their grandma's when she got married. When she died, Mom got it. It had been in their room forever, so both of them have gotten used to standing in weird poses in order to see all of themselves.

Jenni cocked her hip and tilted her head as she ran her hands up her sides to close her fingers around her own throat. Steve liked to do that when they were fooling around. It made her feel woozy and dangerous, and even though he'd never really scared her, part of her was always waiting to be frightened. Part of her wanted to be. She pressed her thumbs against her throat and her eyelids fluttered closed as warmth spread upward from low in her belly.

"Where did you meet a guy that old? The diner?"

Jenni's eyes snapped open at the question, and any desire she'd fleetingly had to give away the necklace vanished with her annoyance at Allie's nosiness. Jenni had been working at the diner since she got her driver's license, which was about the same time she started growing distant and irritable about everything that happened in this little house. With her little friends. Their little lives. The people — the men — who stopped at the diner were almost always on their way to someplace else. Someplace, any place better than Quarrytown.

She'd met *him* at the diner.

Jenni turned with another toss of her hair. The heat in her belly had rushed to her face at the way Allie was staring, but Jenni shook it off. "What do you care? Ilya said bring beer, I'm bringing beer. What difference does it make to you what I had to do to get it?"

"Jennilynn! What *did* you have to do?" Allie squealed.

"Jesus, Alicia. Enough with the Spanish Inquisition. I met a guy, he's old enough to get beer, and he likes me enough to bring it to the party. Quit acting like this is some kind of big deal, because it's not." Jenni turned to face the mirror again, pursing her lips and turning her face from side to side. More blush? More eyeliner. What would Ilya say if she showed up in full-on Goth?

What did she care what fucking Ilya Stern thought about anything? Jenni scowled at her reflection. Not a damned thing, not now or in the future.

"What's going on with you lately?" Allie demanded.

Jenni looked at her sister in the reflection, then once again turned to face her. Slowly, this time. Without the flounce. Again, Jenni remembered how close they'd been. If only she could trust Allie not to run to their folks if Jenni told her the truth…but no. She couldn't trust her little sister with anything like that. Not if she wanted to keep doing what she'd been doing. Not if she wanted to get away with it. That was the trouble with secrets, wasn't it? You had to keep them all by yourself.

"Nothing." Jenni put on a vacant smile. Allie didn't believe her, Jenni could see that. She also knew her sister wasn't going to press her for answers. "It's going to be a slammin' party. Don't be such a loser."

The "L" Jenni made with her thumb and first finger pressed to her forehead was meant to be a joke, but Allie clearly didn't take it that way. She frowned. "We're going to get in trouble."

"Not unless someone narcs on us. Mom and Dad won't be back until late Sunday. Galina's working a double or something. Ilya said she won't be home until morning. Barry went fishing for the weekend. And Babulya's staying with some friends in Camp Hill, some kind of quilting thing."

Galina, Ilya and Niko's mom, worked a lot of nights and weekends. Her still-newish husband Barry was also often away during the same times. Jenni and Allie's parents, however, went away for the weekend only occasionally, and never before without having someone come to stay with them. Galina's mother, Babulya, was almost never gone. If there was ever a time to have a party, this weekend was it.

Allie wasn't satisfied. "What if someone calls the cops?"

"Who's going to call the cops?" Jenni rolled her eyes so hard she swore she could see her own asshole. "We're the only houses on this dead-end street."

Allie left the room. Jenni checked her pager. Steve hadn't sent a message, but she hadn't expected him to. He was out of town. There *was* a message from Dillon, the guy who was supposed to be getting her the beer. Downstairs in the kitchen, she called him back.

"I'll bring it to the party," he said.

He wasn't invited to the party, but Jenni didn't say so. If that was the only way to get him to bring the beer, fine. She rolled her eyes, though. Dillon was a loser, one she didn't feel bad about using to get what she wanted.

Allie had been lingering, listening. "Who was that?"

"Beer delivery," Jenni said with a grin and a toss of her hair. "C'mon. Let's go over."

Chapter 3
REBECCA

Then

It was going to be the party of the year.

Rebecca Segal didn't hang out much with the kids who lived on Quarry Street, even though they'd all gone to school together since kindergarten. The Stern and Harrison families were tight with each other, their own little club, and although Rebecca had imagined Ilya Stern's mouth on hers a hundred times, well, so had almost every other girl in school. Fantasizing about Ilya was pointless, since he had eyes only for Jennilynn Harrison, anyway.

Besides, Rebecca had been going out with Richard Goldman practically since her bat mitzvah, when her parents had insisted they share the celebratory kiddush at the synagogue. Their birthdays were only a week apart. Their dads did business together. Her parents liked and approved of him, and if the Stern brothers had the bad boy swagger and good looks that turned girls' heads, Richie had…well, Richie had money. Or at least his parents did. He also had a car. And a good future, according to Rebecca's mom and dad, who liked to talk about "a good future" a lot.

It was inevitable that they'd end up together. In Quarrytown, there were only a handful of Jewish families. Rebecca's parents had never forbidden her from dating someone who wasn't Jewish, but they sure had made it much easier to date Richie than anyone else — curfews and other rules seemed to fly out the window if they thought she was with him. So, she told her parents she was with him, and most of the time, she was.

Richie didn't hang around the Sterns or Harrisons too much either, but tonight it didn't matter, because the word was out that both sets of adults in the only two houses on the end of Quarry Street were out of town. The news had been shared in whispers and giggles and in notes folded into triangles and passed along the rows of desks in all the classrooms at good old QHS.

It was going to be hella good. A dark thing like a flower unfurled inside her, sending its tendrils into every nook and cranny. It was going to be wild. It was going to be…bad, Rebecca thought and stared at her reflection, watching to see if anything showed in her expression. All she saw was blankness. No hint of the excitement bubbling inside her. No sign that she intended to get wasted tonight. That she was going to dance until she couldn't breathe. Laugh with girls she usually didn't give the time of day to, maybe flirt with boys who had no chance with her.

Maybe she'd finally let Richie do all the things he kept trying to do, or maybe she would make him do to her everything she'd been imagining she wanted. Whatever might happen tonight was going to be a big deal. It was going to change everything.

"Meeting Richie for dinner and a movie, but then I'm

going to sleep over at Libby's." Rebecca twirled her car keys in her hand.

They belonged to the baby blue Volkswagen Cabriolet in the garage. It had been a sweet sixteen gift. She was one of the few girls in her class who had her own ride. One of the few kids in the entire school who had a brand-new car, not a hand-me-down. Even Richie drove his mother's old Volvo. Rebecca kind of hated the Cabriolet. It had made her popular, and that wasn't so bad, except that most of the girls who'd started asking her to hang out with them were only doing it so she'd give them rides to the mall. It was better than having to beg for rides herself, though.

"Libby's?" Rebecca's mom tipped her head down to peer over her reading glasses. Her lips pursed. "If I call Richard's mother, will he also be having a sleepover with 'a friend?'"

"I don't know, Mother, maybe you should," Rebecca answered coolly.

Considering the way her parents seemed bent on shoving her down the aisle with Richie even though they were both just barely eighteen, the fact that her mother was even pretending to be worried about them sleeping together was irritating. Besides. They weren't. Richie had, so far, been satisfied with an occasional handjob and had never even asked her to put it in her mouth.

Linda Segal harrumphed but bent back to the needlework in her lap. She'd been working on the same piece for the past six months. Now she sighed and pulled out a pair of tiny scissors to rip free a few threads.

Rebecca waited for more questions, but her mom seemed satisfied with the lie. For a moment, just one, Rebecca wished her mom wouldn't let it go. She wanted to spill everything. The party. The drinking she planned to do. The trouble she wanted to get into.

"I'll be home tomorrow," Rebecca said.

Her mom looked up again, taking in Rebecca's pegged jeans and oversized men's shirt, along with the tie hung loosely around her throat. "Would it kill you to dress up once in a while? For a date, at least?"

"I like this outfit."

"I'm sure you do, but what does Richard think about it?"

Rebecca rolled her eyes. "I'll ask him and let you know."

"Becky-boo, don't be like that."

Rebecca didn't protest the childhood nickname. It usually made her grit her teeth. Tonight, for some reason, it made her feel like crying and hugging her mom, something she hadn't done in...well, in a long time.

"Richie likes the way I dress," she said, although she honestly had no idea what he thought about the way she dressed and really didn't care.

Her mom rolled her eyes but smiled. "Have a good time. Tell Libby's mom I said hi."

Guilt. It didn't last long. Excitement overtook it.

At the pizza shop where she'd agreed to meet Richie, he paid for a couple of slices for each of them. His had pepperoni, which he ate with a super smug grin on his face. Lips covered with grease. His mother would've had a fit if she'd known he was eating *treif*. Rebecca didn't care much, one way or the other. Her parents didn't keep anything close to kosher, but the Goldmans did.

"You gonna finish that?" He jabbed a finger at her pizza.

She pushed it across the table with a shrug. "What time do you want to leave?"

"Whenever." Richie shrugged and looked up, still

chewing. He frowned around the mouthful. "You're serious, right? You really want to go? It's just a lame party."

It was so much more than that, but she wasn't going to try to convince him of it. "You don't have to go if you don't want to."

"We could go back to my house. My parents are out for the night."

She stopped her lip from curling. "I told a bunch of people I'd be there. But like I said, you don't have to go."

"Could be fun." Richie shrugged again.

She didn't want him to go to the party. She hadn't thought much about it before, assuming he'd come along because he was her boyfriend, and it was what she wanted to do, and since he was her boyfriend he would go along with it. But she really hadn't wanted him to come, and now with the possibility that he might ditch the party, it was all she could think about. Going to the party to drink and smoke and dance and…flirt, yeah. All of that, without Richie.

She couldn't think of a way to say so. Hell, she could barely permit herself to think it. Before Rebecca had a chance to blurt out something stupid, Richie guzzled the rest of his soda and stifled a belch behind his hand.

"Benji wanted to hang out tonight anyway," he said.

Hang out meant playing video games and who knew, watching soft-core porn. But it was an out, and while there'd been times in the past when Rebecca would've been a bitch about it, tonight she simply shrugged the way he had. Richie burped again.

"I'll just go and hang out with Madison and those guys," Rebecca said. "Have fun with Benji."

Chapter 4
JENNI

Then

With her parents barely two hours on the road, Jenni was wasted and dancing so hard in the center of the Sterns' living room that her halter dress could barely stay up. Dillon, who'd bought her the case of beer, showed up to the party with an additional couple bottles of rum. He was way too old to be at a high school party, but nobody seemed to notice, and he sure as hell didn't care. The Stern brothers pulled out a stash of vodka. Ilya was mixing some with red punch. Someone else spilled the chips all over the living room floor and kids danced on them, crushing them into the carpet.

Someone put on that song by the Violent Femmes, the one about just one kiss. Jenni didn't know all the words, but she shouted along with everyone else as the room erupted into a seething mass of kids jumping in unison. The pictures rattled on the walls. Someone knocked over a lamp. Niko and Allie were nowhere to be found, the little shits. Jenni searched the room for Ilya, but she couldn't find him, either.

In the bathroom she threw up, mostly into the toilet, and rinsed her mouth. She spit in the sink. Her reflection showed sweaty hair, rings of dark smudge beneath her eyes. She bared her teeth, outlined in red from the vodka punch, and laughed in her own fucking face.

"Hey, babe." Dillon rapped on the door and opened it without waiting for her say anything. "You okay?"

"Better out than in," she said.

When he kissed her, backing her up against the wall, she knew she shouldn't let him. He was a creep. He was too old for her. He was a shady character, the type of guy who'd buy underage kids beer and make out with a high school student when he was closer to thirty than twenty. It wasn't like she'd lied about her age, either. But that wasn't why she shouldn't let him kiss her. She had other reasons for that, and a shiver went through her at the thought of what Steve would do if he knew she was fooling around with another guy.

He'd be angry, wouldn't he? Jealous? He might even get a little rough with her. Jenni shivered again.

"Want to get out of here?" Dillon asked.

Jenni broke the kiss and turned her head. "This is like, my party. I can't just leave it."

"So, we'll go out back. For a little bit."

She knew what *that* meant. "You need something?"

"Couple of things," Dillon said with a smile. "Things that'll make me feel real, real good. Maybe you, too."

"Already feeling good."

Dillon kissed her again, tongue sliding between her lips. For a second she almost thought she was going to puke again, and what would Dillon do if she blew chunks into his mouth? Jenni giggled at that, and he pulled away to look at her face. His eyes narrowed.

"Something funny?"

Jenni shook her head. The vodka punch and the beer had warmed her. Made her dozy. Happy. It was so hard to be happy, anymore. She was never happy.

Jenni was almost, almost always sad.

"Come out back with me." Dillon took her by the wrist to tug her out the door. "We'll have our own little party."

In the backyard, Jenni caught sight of two shadowy figures near the picnic table. The Sterns' backyard was overgrown, thick with dead brown weeds. The music from the house covered up anything the people sitting out there were saying, but it didn't look like they were speaking anyway. It was Allie, Jenni saw as Dillon tugged her around the side of the house, toward the tree line and the path that led toward the quarry. Allie and…Niko?

"What the hell?" Jenni mumbled, but Dillon pulled her away before she could get a positive glimpse.

Dillon held her up as she tripped. He kissed her again. His big hands settled on her hips, pinching.

"What've you got for me?" He nuzzled her neck.

"No marks," she told him. Dillon was trying to give her a hickey, like he was sixteen instead of however the hell old he really was.

"Someone else doesn't seem to have the same rules." He touched the faint purple marks on her neck.

She knocked his hand away. "That's none of your goddamned business."

"Hey, hey, listen, it's not like I care if you're getting some on the side. Or hell, it's not like I care if I'm the some on the side. But if you don't want marks, you'd better tell whoever the other guy is."

"There's no other guy." The denial was automatic out of habit.

Dillon didn't seem to care. He wheedled, "C'mon, baby, I need a little something."

Of course he did. Dillon had been buying from Barry since before Jenni got recruited to expand the market. He was her best customer.

Jenni inched out of his embrace. She wasn't sober, and she didn't want to be, but she was losing at least the edge of her drunkenness. She patted her hip and let out a laugh.

"Oops. Forgot. No pockets." She spread the hem of her dress, almost losing her balance again.

"Damn it!"

"Relax," she told him with a scowl. "I have some at home. I just have to walk over and get them."

"I'll come with you."

They walked across the street, which had been lined with cars for the past hour or so. Inside her house, she told Dillon to wait in the kitchen while she ran upstairs to grab the small mint tin in which she kept the supply of painkillers she sold. She was almost out. She'd have to get some more from Barry. He'd want his cash soon, too, and she double checked to make sure that was safe in its hiding place too. It would suck if Allie or worse, her mom, found it.

Before going back downstairs to trade the pills to Dillon for some money, Jenni checked her pager. Nothing. She tucked the pager away in her underwear drawer. Disappointment reminded her of the taste of vomit. In her bathroom she brushed her teeth. Spat. Brushed, rinsed, spat again.

Steve had told her he'd be on the road for a few days, maybe a week. He'd told her he wasn't coming to a high school party anyway, even if he was home. If Dillon was way too old to be there, Steve was literally old enough to be the father to most if not all of the kids are the party. Including Jenni.

Steve wasn't her father, though. He was something else that had no name. He was another of her secrets, and she held it tight to herself.

Chapter 5
REBECCA

Then

The music was so loud that Rebecca couldn't hear anything Madison was saying, but it probably didn't matter. The other girl was already so drunk that she could hardly stand up. It was gross. Rebecca had barely managed to finish one plastic cup of warm, fizzy beer. Her stomach was already upset. So much for partying hard.

"Tristan," Madison finally said into Rebecca's ear.

"Huh?"

Madison nudged Rebecca's shoulder, then pointed toward the corner where a group of guys were gathered around a beer pong setup. "Tristan Weatherfield!"

Rebecca looked again. She knew Tristan, of course. Quarry High was so small that everyone knew everyone else, because most of them had been in class together since kindergarten. She knew Tristan, but they'd never hung out. Tristan wore black leather jackets and spiked his dark hair. He had a James Dean kind of retro vibe mixed up with a punk/rockabilly Stray Cats style, and guys like him didn't pay girls like Rebecca the time of day. She was the Steff to his Andie in their school's version of *Pretty in Pink*. Different worlds. Different universes, as a matter of fact.

"He's cute!" Madison breathed beer-scented breath into Rebecca's face. "He keeps looking at you."

Rebecca attempted another sip from the red plastic cup, trying to hide the shudder of disgust at the beer's sour flavor. "Maybe he's looking at *you*."

"You think so?" Madison waved a hand, jangling her armful of bracelets. "Should I go ask him to dance or something?"

"I don't think this is the sort of party where you do that."

"Right, right." Madison looked serious. "You should do it, then."

Rebecca laughed, her attention caught away from the cute rebel boy in the corner to Jennilynn Harrison, who was being led away by the stranger none of them knew. The guy was old. At least thirty. Good-looking, but in a shady way.

"Go." Madison shoved her.

Rebecca took a couple of stumbling steps toward the group of boys. Tristan wasn't looking at her, so he didn't see how clumsy she was. On the other hand, he wasn't looking at *her*, which meant that Madison was just too drunk to know what the hell she was talking about.

The beer in Rebecca's cup sloshed. So much for her getting drunk and wild tonight. She should have gone out with Richie. She could have let him take her back to his house, where they'd have tussled on the couch in the basement rumpus room. He'd have tried to get her shirt off like that was some big deal, to see her boobs. She'd have let him after a struggle, not because she really thought it was a big deal, but because good girls held out.

"Tired of being a good girl," she said.

Madison blinked. "Huh? What?"

"Nothing. Never mind." Rebecca steeled herself, then tossed back the contents of her cup. She grimaced at the nasty taste, but welcomed the warmth spreading through her. She handed the empty to Madison.

She had to weave her way through a group of kids dirty dancing on top of a bunch of potato chips being crushed into the carpet, but she kept going. By the time she got to where Tristan was standing, she expected to lose her nerve. To her own surprise though, Rebecca put herself squarely in front of him.

"Hi, Tristan."

Tristan turned and gave her a long, obvious look, up and down. "Hey."

"Rebecca," she said. "Segal. We had Bio II together last year."

"I guess so." His eyes were red. His stance and his grin were both a little wobbly. He focused on her, but barely, as he took a long swig. "Where's your drink?"

"I guess I need a new one. Want to get one with me?" Her own boldness shocked her. Maybe the beer she'd managed to chug *was* affecting her.

Tristan drained his cup by tipping back his head. Rebecca watched, fascinated, at how the muscles of his throat worked. When he finished, giving her another of those wobbly grins, her stomach tightened and a hot flush crept up her throat into her cheeks.

Drinks had been set out in the kitchen. Empty bottles lined the counter. The trashcan was already overflowing with discarded red plastic cups. The floor, sticky from spilled red fruit punch. Ilya and Niko's mother was going to be super pissed when she got home. Rebecca couldn't imagine ever throwing a party like this at her house.

Tristan pulled two cups from the top of the trash and ran them under the kitchen faucet before turning to her. "Punch!"

"Sure." She wasn't going to be grossed out by the fact he took them from the trash, Rebecca told herself. She was carefree, loose as a goose, she was totally chill.

Tristan poured them both cups of punch. He held up his cup to knock against hers. "Cheers."

Drinking the punch was like taking a punch, right to the guts. It was so much worse than the beer. Rebecca shuddered with disgust at the vodka's strong taste, barely cut at all by the equally disgusting red punch. Tristan saw her grimace and laughed.

"The more you drink, the better it tastes," he said.

She was already noticing that. She sipped again. The music wasn't as loud in here, but while that would make conversation easier, she was having a hard time figuring out what to say.

"You sat in the back," Tristan said suddenly.

Rebecca's eyebrows lifted before understanding what he meant. "Oh. Yeah."

"I remember you now."

It didn't sound flattering, but it was better than him having no idea who she was. Tristan gave her another of those up-and-down looks. She tried not to blush.

"Rebecca Segal," he said. "You and Richie go together."

She took a long drink, forcing herself not to show how horrible it was. She kept her answer nonchalant. "Yeah. I guess so."

"He's not here."

"No," Rebecca told him.

Tristan smiled. "Sweet."

Rebecca was not expecting the kiss. Sloppy and

sudden, it almost missed her mouth. Tristan's body against hers made her stumble back so that her hip hit the table. Bottles rattled again. Faster than she'd have thought him capable of grabbing her, he snagged her wrist to keep her from falling.

"Easy," Tristan said. "Sorry?"

"Don't be."

This time, she kissed him, and Rebecca wasn't sure if it was the beer and the shitty punch or the fact she'd been aching to do something like this for what felt like her entire life. She didn't care, and it didn't matter. Tristan's mouth was on hers, and his tongue was sweeping inside it, and she felt giddy and free and *alive*.

"You want to go find a place?" Tristan asked her.

Rebecca's heart thudded so hard she felt a little faint. "Yeah. Sure."

Chapter 6
JENNI

Then

Dillon had been satisfied enough by the pills Jenni had given him, but when she demanded he pay for them, he refused. They'd argued. He seemed to think that because he'd bought her beer and liquor that somehow made them equal.

"No tradesies," she told him, wishing she wasn't sobering up.

"Look, you little bitch. I brought you and your underage friends the booze you asked for. I thought we had an understanding, and that was that you'd have something for me. Which meant giving it to me, not making me pay for it."

"Everyone pays for it," she retorted. "That's how it works, you dumbass."

"You are a nasty little whore."

His words stung, even though she tried not to let them. "Yeah? And you're a pathetic old fuck with a drug problem. I could get beer anywhere, but you can't get what I have from just anyone."

"You think it's cool, huh? Playing games with me?" He shook his head and spat to the side.

In the shadows along the side of the Stern house, Jenni could hear the music from inside. She wanted to go back inside the party and forget this old dude and the pills for tonight. She never sold to kids in her class. She wanted to drink some more, dance some more. She pushed Dillon back with both hands square on his chest.

"Fuck off, creep."

When he made to grab at her, she ducked away from his fumbling and punched him in the face. It was luck on her part; she'd swung wildly. When he grunted and stepped back, though, Jenni held up her fists again.

"I said, 'fuck off.'"

Dillon held up his hands. "Fine. Jesus."

"And if you ever fucking put your hands on me again," she added, "I'll make sure you never get to buy anything from me or my supplier ever again."

This last bit was pure brash bluffing. She doubted Barry would let a sale go, especially from a regular like this guy. It felt good to see him look nervous, though. Sure, he could probably get his drugs from somewhere else, but Barry, and therefore Jenni, were both known to have high quality shit at prices even a non-desperate addict could consider fair. She had deliveries on the regular, too. Consistent.

"Good luck getting high when you have to suck a dick so you can get your Jackpot," she told him, referring to one of the street names for at least one of the drugs she'd been selling.

"Fuck you." Dillon shot this over his shoulder as he stalked around the corner of the house and out of sight.

Jenni sagged against the side of the house. If she hadn't been sober before, the adrenaline throbbing through her was making her feel like she was. She needed more to drink.

The figure loomed out of the shadows in front of her so suddenly she screamed. In the next instant she swatted at him. "Ilya! God, you scared me!"

"Sorry. You okay?"

"I'm fine. I need something to drink. I want to dance." She punched at his arm, but lightly this time. Softer.

He grabbed her wrist and held it. She didn't try to pull away. Then, in the shadows, Ilya moved closer.

She kissed him, pushing up a bit on her toes to do it. "Hi."

"Hi," he said.

Their foreheads pressed together. The music from inside the house had switched from something raucous to a slower song. She and Ilya moved together in a slow dance. Jenni's head went onto his shoulder.

"Who's the douchebag?" His question sounded almost conversational, but Jenni knew better. Ilya was trying too hard to sound like he didn't care.

"Nobody."

"Did he hurt you?"

She pulled away to look at his face, still half in shadow so that she could only guess at the rest of his features. "No."

"If he did —"

"He didn't," Jenni said and kissed him again.

"What are you doing, Jenni?" Ilya sounded wary.

She didn't want that, and she didn't want him to be thinking too much about this. She wasn't going to. "Kissing you. C'mon."

"Why are you kissing me?"

She sighed and leaned back against the side of the house with her arms crossed. "Because I want to."

"You're drunk."

"So are you," she told him, tone dripping with scorn. "What difference does *that* make?"

Ilya shook his head. "The party is getting out of control."

"Yeah?"

He grinned. "Yeah."

"Kiss me, Ilya. Kiss me." She breathed the words, and with the music pumping out from inside, it would have been very easy for him not to hear her, or to pretend that he had not.

"Why?" He moved closer to put his hands on her hips. He didn't kiss her.

"Because I want you to."

He sighed and shook his head, but then he did gave her what she wanted. When the kiss broke, he didn't move away from her. His arousal pressed her stomach. Jenni closed her eyes, wishing Steve had paged her. Wishing Ilya had refused to kiss her.

"I want to smoke," she said next.

"I have a couple of joints in my room. But it's all I have, there's not enough to go around."

"So, we won't share." She gave him a grin that felt twisted but must've looked fine, because he let her take his hand and pull him toward the door.

Chapter 7
REBECCA

Then

Rebecca couldn't believe she'd actually followed Tristan upstairs to the attic bedroom, but here she was. He'd turned on the light switch at the bottom of the stairs, but it controlled only the fixture in the stairwell itself. The bedroom was still mostly dark.

She guessed by the clothes strewn about the floor and the poster of a swimsuit model thumbtacked to the attic's sloping, beamed ceiling, that the bedroom belonged to either Ilya or Nikolai, and not their stepsister, Theresa. She'd seen the younger girl laughing and dancing with some underclassmen Rebecca didn't know. She would never have dared go to a senior party before this year, but she guessed that if it was held in the house where you lived, you got the right to invite some of your friends.

"I didn't know you were friends with Ilya," Tristan said.

"I'm not. Jenni and I have study hall together. She invited me."

Tristan nodded. He'd seemed super confident in the kitchen, but now that they were both up here and the bed was prominently the only place to sit, he was acting like he wasn't sure what to do. Rebecca was definitely feeling the red punch.

"I have a boyfriend," she said.

He nodded. "Yeah. Richie. We talked about it."

"I want you to kiss me again."

Tristan smiled. "Even though you have a boyfriend?"

In reply, she stepped closer to him. She offered her mouth, eyes closed. Heart pounding. He took so long to press his mouth to hers that Rebecca had started to think he wasn't going to. Then, the sweet pressure of his lips. The gentle probe of his tongue. She sighed and opened for him. His arms went around her.

Somehow, they ended up on the bed. Arms and legs tangling. Hands groping, moving, roaming.

Rebecca had never been like this with Richie. Their makeout sessions usually ended when he tried to slide his hand up beneath her shirt and she pushed his hand away. He always did and then would stop kissing her.

"...gives up too easy," she murmured into Tristan's mouth.

"What?"

"Nothing." She kissed him harder.

He rolled on top of her. This was going so fast. She didn't care. The room was spinning a little. The bed, a rocking boat on a sea of desire. She wanted this and wanted him, wanted more than small town life and a steady boyfriend her parents had picked out for her.

The sound of footsteps on the stairs didn't register with her until the single overhead bulb came on. Bright as day. It stabbed light into Rebecca's eyes over Tristan's shoulder, and she cried out and threw up a hand to shield them.

Tristan, eyes closed, face flushed with passion, didn't seem to notice at first. At Rebecca's low shout, though, he opened his eyes and strained around to look at who was interrupting them.

"Oh, shit, sorry."

Rebecca didn't recognize the male voice, but through the curve of Tristan's arm she glimpsed a flash of blond curls. Jennilynn. She strained to look and saw Ilya. Rebecca had time to think that was interesting, the two of them together, before she realized she'd been caught.

Tristan seemed to realize it, too. He shielded her from sight with his body. "Sorry, el roomo es occupado."

"Dude, it's my room!"

"Can you come back in about ten minutes?" Tristan asked.

Rebecca heard soft, gruff laughter from Ilya. "Sure, if that's only how long you can last."

"C'mon," Jennilynn said. "Let's get out of here."

When they'd gone, turning the light off too, Tristan sat up. "Oops."

Her stomach was churning, only this time not with lustful anticipation. Richie didn't hang around with Ilya, but he and Jennilynn had a bunch of classes together, and Rebecca didn't trust the other girl not to spill the beans. She was know for being a little bitchy, a side of her Rebecca had witnessed but never experienced personally, since she had the same sort of reputation.

"Hey. You okay?"

Rebecca hadn't realized she was shaking until Tristan touched her shoulder. She shook her head, not trusting herself to speak. If she opened her mouth, she would cry. Or puke.

"They couldn't see you," he said as though he knew exactly her reasons for being scared.

She shook her head and gulped down a sour runnel of spit. "Are you sure?"

"Yeah. I'm sure. Anyway, they were both pretty wasted." Tristan shifted so they could both sit up next to each other.

"I should go."

He made a small noise and put a hand on her knee. "Wait."

"Really, I shouldn't have come up here with you," she began, but he squeezed her knee and she fell silent.

"You said you wanted me to kiss you."

"I did."

Tristan looked serious. "I'm not going to tell anyone. I mean, Richie or anything. I won't tell him."

"Thanks. Still, I shouldn't have come up here with you, or kissed you…or anything else."

"You must've had a reason," he said.

Rebecca closed her eyes for a second. She drew in a slow breath. The floor felt slanted under her toes, even though she knew it wasn't.

"I just…wanted something different," she told him, trying to explain something she wasn't quite sure she understood herself.

"I'm something different?"

"Yes." She opened her eyes. "You're something very different, Tristan."

Chapter 8
JENNI

Then

On Monday, school was abuzz with stories of the blowout party that had happened over the weekend. Rumors were growing, spread by kids who hadn't been invited or who'd stupidly passed up the chance to attend, some of them confirmed and exaggerated by kids who'd been there to make themselves look cooler. Jenni herself had been asked point-blank if it was true that the undercover cop at the party had been convinced not to bust anyone because he'd been given a blowie by an unnamed freshman. She'd said yes.

Jenni had already been a princess at school. Popular, although she knew it wasn't because she was well-liked. Other girls tried to be like her. Guys wanted to get with her. She knew about her bitchy reputation, and it had never bothered her because it was at least a little true. Now, though, the stories of the epic party spread and grew, launching Jenni into the realm of superstar.

Only one thing had happened that she was a little

worried about, and she was going to confront Rebecca Segal about it right away. Jenni found her in study hall, sixth period. Miss Delaney was notorious for taking a very long bathroom break at the beginning of this period, leaving her study hall unattended. So long as everyone kept the noise down none of the other teachers seemed to notice, and most of the kids used the time to gossip and chat rather than study.

"Hey." Jenni slid into the desk next to Rebecca.

Rebecca had been reading a book and making notes on the pulpy gray notepad the school provided at the start of every month. She looked up, eyes narrowed, her smile insincere. "Hi."

"I want to talk to you about the party." Jenni leaned forward so nobody could overhear them. "You better not tell anyone about me."

The other girl blinked and furrowed her brow. "About…you?"

"Don't play stupid," Jenni hissed. "I know you were in Ilya's room with Tristan. I know you saw us going up there. You'd better not spread any rumors about me and him. That's all."

"Why would I?" Rebecca looked pissed off. She also leaned forward, dropping her voice. "You'd better not say anything about me being there, either."

"Mutually assured destruction," Jenni told her with a grimace.

Rebecca nodded and sat back. "Yeah. Okay. Anyway, I wouldn't say anything about it. It was a party. People do dumb things at parties like that."

"I just don't want anyone thinking me and Ilya are more than friends." Jenni hated the way her throat had closed up and the burning of tears behind her eyelids.

Why did she care so damned much? So what if

Rebecca told the whole school that she and Ilya had been going to his bedroom, which she wouldn't, because doing so would give up her own secrets, and Jenni ought to have known that. Why did she care so much about any of it?

"I won't say anything to anyone." Rebecca looked concerned. "Are you all right?"

Jenni was not all right. The party had ended days ago, but Jenni still felt hungover. Colors too harsh, lights too bright. She'd fidgeted her way through the first five periods today. Couldn't sit still. Couldn't wait to get out of school. She had to work the evening shift at the diner tonight, already had some deliveries scheduled. Cash money.

Maybe she'd see Steve.

The thought of that quieted her. "I'm fine. Just know that if you do say anything, I will end you."

"Jeeze, fine, okay." Rebecca frowned and shook her head. "I get it."

For a fleeting second, Jenni felt bad. She and Rebecca had never been friends, but they hadn't been enemies, either. Until Jenni had recognized her under Tristan in Ilya's bed, she'd never have given the other girl even a passing thought. Now, though, they seemed inextricably linked by the fact that both of them had witnessed the other doing something neither one wanted anyone else to know.

Without another word, Jenni got up from the desk and went back to her own just as Ms. Delaney came into the room. "Okay, class, settle. Settle. Who needs library passes?"

Hands went up, including Rebecca's. Jenni had no reason to visit the library. She looked out the window instead. As a half dozen kids filed up for passes, she put her head in one hand and pretended she was busy taking notes.

Truth was, she might try to grab a nap. There was only half an hour left in the period.

She slept.

She dreamed.

Last Summer

"She says they're going to get married!"

Ilya paced in Jenni's den. Her parents were still at work, and Allie was upstairs in her room with the radio playing loud. Summer vacation had just started, but already they were bored, wanting to get into trouble. He and Jenni had planned to smoke a little weed and watch some shitty scary movies, the kind with a lot of bare bouncing boobs and blood.

Jenni hadn't been expecting Ilya to drop this bomb. "She's going to marry *that* guy? The one from the hospital?"

"Barry Malone. Yeah. That's what she says. Next month. Talk about short notice." Ilya threw himself onto the couch beside her.

"Maybe she's knocked up," Jenni said and ducked away from the cushion he used to hit her. "Stop it, jerk!"

Ilya didn't laugh. "You wouldn't be laughing if it was *your* mother."

"Awww. Poor puppy."

Jenni had some problems with her folks, but nothing like Ilya and Niko had to handle with their mom, Galina. She was crazy. Like, literally. But Jenni couldn't tell him that. She didn't have to tell him, Ilya knew it. But she couldn't say it to him, because he was so clearly upset.

They'd been friends for so long, all their lives, it felt

like. When she gestured for him to come closer, he gave in to her embrace. She petted his hair. The kiss happened almost by accident, although later Jenni would have to admit to herself that she'd been thinking about trying that out for a long time.

Somehow she was on his lap, his face in her hands and her mouth on his. They kissed and kissed and kissed, and she ground herself against him. Ilya pushed up against her, turned them both until they were on the couch with him between her legs, they moved and rocked together, and it was better than anything she'd ever felt before, with anyone. Ever.

She went still at the sound he made. Heat flooded between them and when he pulled away, a small dark spot had bloomed on the front of his jeans. Jenni didn't know what to do about that. She knew what it meant, obviously, but not how they'd gone so far, so fast. What did this mean for them now?

Ilya wasn't looking at her. He shifted, tugging at the crotch of his jeans. Jenni didn't want him to regret this. She didn't, did she? She couldn't even be sure of her own feelings about this, only that everything had changed between them, and it was suddenly weird. Too weird.

"Hey, let's go to the fireman's carnival," she said abruptly. "My mom left me some money to order a pizza for dinner, but if we let Allie come with us, we can use it there. Call Niko. Babulya will drive us, won't she?"

"She wouldn't have to, if you got your license already," he told her.

Jenni made a face. Ilya didn't have his license yet, either. "Jerk."

"Bitch," he said, but fondly.

Maybe it would be okay.

At the carnival, the four of them gorged on junk food

and rode a few of the rickety rides. Allie and Niko broke off to go find funnel cakes, but Jenni stopped in front of the game booth decorated with gigantic grinning goldfish.

"You want one?" It was just about the first thing Ilya had said to her since they'd gotten off the couch.

It took him a couple tries, but at last he sunk a ping-pong ball into one of the small fish bowls. Jenni held up the plastic baggie, the water swirling with fish poop. Inside, a gold and black fish gaped at her.

"I'm going to name him Chester," she said and kissed Ilya on the cheek.

Some time after that, she tossed poor old Chester into the quarry, and not long after *that*, she went over to the Sterns' house one day when Galina's car was not in the driveway. Allie had gone to the library. Jenni had been looking for Ilya, but she'd found Galina's new husband, instead.

Jenni startled herself awake just before the bell signaling the end of class rang. Embarrassed, she looked around to see if anyone had noticed her sleeping. Nobody seemed to.

Dreaming about that first time with Ilya left her with an unsettled feeling in her gut. He'd won her that goldfish, and she'd tossed it in the quarry. Galina and Barry had married shortly after that in a no-frills ceremony that seemed to have taken everyone by surprise except the two of them. Jenni had gone on to finally get her driver's license. Then the job at the diner. She'd started working for Barry, exchanging the pills for money.

She and Ilya...well. What the hell were they, anyway? She hadn't known that first time at the beginning of the summer. She still didn't know.

Pagers had been forbidden at school, but hers was in her purse, wrapped up in a pair of thick socks to keep the buzz muffled. She checked it now, surreptitiously. At the sight of a message, her heart leaped. She couldn't stop herself from grinning even as she tucked it back into her bag.

Steve was back in town. He wanted to see her. Jenni trembled at the thought of it, and that made it easier to stop thinking about Ilya altogether.

Chapter 9
REBECCA

Then

The note in Rebecca's locker wasn't signed, but she knew immediately who'd left it there. Scrawled in a loose, looping hand, the note contained only a phone number. She tucked it into the pocket of her jeans just as Richie came up behind her to put an arm around her shoulders.

"Cut it out." She shrugged out of his grasp with a frown.

"Why?"

"You can't just come up to me and grab me like that," Rebecca told him. "It's gross."

Richie looked offended. "Sorry. I just thought, being that you're my girlfriend and all...."

"That doesn't give you the right to just grab me whenever you feel like it." This was the first time she'd seen him since Saturday evening, when they'd parted ways. Usually they met in the mornings to walk the school halls before homeroom, but today she'd "overslept."

He couldn't see it on her, the fact she'd made out with Tristan. He couldn't know she'd fallen asleep in the back seat of Tristan's car, or that he'd driven her home in the first blush of dawn, before her parents woke up. The only person who might have a clue was Jennilynn, and she wasn't going to say anything to anyone.

He couldn't see her guilt, either, because she wasn't feeling any.

She was going to break up with him. Right now. No explanation, or maybe she'd use the fact he grabbed her as an excuse. Rebecca's mouth opened, ready with the words.

"I'm going over to Benji's house after school today, but Mom wanted me to ask you if you wanted to come to Friday night dinner this week." Richie paused to look apologetic. "She's doing the whole candles and challah thing."

While Rebecca's parents made a point of celebrating all the Jewish holidays, they rarely did the Friday night shabbat dinner. Mrs. Goldman, on the other hand, had decided a few years before that at least once a month, the family would do "the candles and challah thing," a Friday night dinner with all the traditional blessings and fanfare. Sometimes she invited Rebecca's parents, too.

Sure enough, the next words out of Richie's mouth were "she says to ask your mom and dad if they want to come."

She was trapped. A rising misery throttled her as easily as a fist squeezing her throat. She and Richie were a couple. Her parents liked him. His liked her.

Her mother would not approve of Tristan Weatherfield. Not Jewish, but worse than that, *poor*. His parents were even rumored not to be divorced, but to have never been married in the first place.

"Sure. Friday night," she said. "I'll ask them."

"Am I a terrible person?" She posed this question to Tristan later that night, after she'd dialed the number on the note.

She'd thought it would reach a pager, but it rang to his house. He'd answered on the second ring. She'd almost hung up without even saying hello.

"For kissing me?"

"Yes. For not breaking up with him. For saying I would go to his house for dinner but now, calling you." Rebecca blew out a breath into the darkness. She had her own phone line in her room, so there were no worries that one of her parents would pick up the line and overhear anything she was saying.

"I don't think you calling me makes you a terrible person, Rebecca."

She didn't say anything for a second or so. "What about the rest of it? What if you were Richie? What would you think?"

"I could never be Richie," Tristan said in a tone of such disdain that it took her aback.

"What's the supposed to mean?"

"Whatever you want it to mean."

That wasn't an answer. She waited another few seconds, listening to the sound of his breathing through line. She thought he'd hang up on her. He didn't.

"No," she whispered. "You could never be Richie."

Chapter 10
JENNI

Last Summer

Nobody was supposed to swim in the quarry, of course. Kids had drowned in it, at least that was the story, although Jenni couldn't honestly remember ever hearing about any real kids who'd died there. The cops patrolled the beach side of it regularly, mostly to catch the kids who were parking along the dead-end road that led to it. They didn't pay much attention to this side, the cliff side, which could be reached through the woods that began at the end of Quarry Street.

The group, Ilya, Niko, Allie and Jenni, and now their new comrade in crime, Barry's daughter Theresa, never told their parents they were going swimming. Parents would tell them it wasn't safe. Parents would say they should go to the local pool instead. Parents, though, worked during the day, and what they didn't know couldn't hurt them.

"So...whattya think about Barry?" In her tube, Jenni paddled through the cold water toward her sister. She nudged Alicia until she opened her eyes. "He's pretty creepy, huh?"

Alicia gripped the sides of her raft and glared. What a wimp. "Hey, watch out."

"He is, right?" Jenni nudged her sister again with a red-painted toe, rocking Allie's raft. She grinned. "What are you afraid of, you'll melt or something?"

Alicia gripped the raft so hard it dented the soft rubber. "Stop it. I just don't want to get my hair wet."

Jenni let herself bend in half to dunk herself down through her tube, then resurfaced to end up with her butt in the center with her legs dangling over the sides. She didn't give a damn about her hair getting wet. The sun was bleaching it whiter every day, and she liked it that way. When the roots grew in darker, more like a honey gold color, she wouldn't even try to color them. She was still thinking about dying it some weird color. Or black. There was always going black.

"I know, you're afraid of Chester. You think he's gonna chomp you." She laughed as she said it.

Chester was the carnival goldfish Jenni had tossed in the water a couple weeks ago. Since then, they'd all been joking that he was out there, growing and growing like the sunfish in that movie they watched a few months ago about a mountain where all the animals had mutated because of mercury poisoning or something from a mine.

Allie snorted. "Sure, that's it."

"Answer my question, Allie."

Allie settled back on the raft, though she hooked a foot against her sister's to keep them from floating away from each other and to keep Jenni from tipping her. "About Chester?"

"Noooo. About Galina's new husband." Jenni rolled her eyes.

"I dunno. He seemed okay at the wedding. He's been nice to us so far." Allie shrugged.

Barry Malone had married Galina before any of them had barely known she had a serious boyfriend. It had kind of fucked up Ilya. Then again, Ilya was kind of fucked up in general. Jenni looked across the water to where he was laying on the outcropping of rock where they kept their towels. On his back, shades protecting his eyes from the sun, probably napping. Even at this distance, she could see the defined muscles of his biceps. Imagined his abs. She shuddered and hated herself for wanting him.

"Theresa's okay, I guess," Jenni said, forcing her attention from Ilya to the girl reading next to him. His new stepsister, Barry's daughter, a bit younger than all of them. She'd fallen into their little group easily enough. "Can you imagine, though? Having to actually *live* with those guys?"

"At least she doesn't have to share a room," Allie said.

"No shit," Jenni agreed with another grin. "Sharing a room totally sucks."

Allie laughed and shoved Jenni's tube with her toes, but Jenni was too fast and grabbed Allie's ankle so she didn't tip. Also so the force of Allie's shove didn't force them apart. Jenni dug her nails in a little too deep, though.

"Ouch!"

"Sorry," Jenni said.

They floated in silence for a few minutes. Chilly water lapped at Jenni's toes. Her butt was getting numb, not just from the temperature of the water but also because of the way she had to contort herself to fit inside it. She had a fat ass, she thought lazily, but knew it wasn't true. Even though she'd started eating pie after every shift at the diner, she wasn't anything close to fat. Thinking of the diner now, she also thought of Barry.

"You're a natural at this," Barry had told her.

Barry had been selling his own shit for some time before she met him, but recruiting Jenni had been a smart move. Men would pay a pretty girl more than they would give another dude, even if they didn't realize it. More money for him. More money for her. Jenni was all about more money, since the more she had, the sooner she could get out of this place. Get away. Far, far away.

And then what?

"I don't know what I want to be when I grow up," Jenni said suddenly, aloud. She wanted to bite the words back at once, but too late. There they were, out in the world.

Allie didn't open her eyes. "Who says you have to?"

"Everyone has to decide at some point, Allie. You can't just screw around forever. You have to decide." Jenni shook her head and then let it fall back so her hair draped into the water. Weighting her. She imagined Chester the goldfish coming for a nibble, tugging her backward, out of the tube. Under the water.

How long would it take for her to drown?

"But not right now." Allie sounded sleepy. If she wasn't careful, she was going to get a sunburn. "It's not like the world will end if you don't."

"Easy for you to say. Nobody's counting on you to make them proud."

The sudden splash swamped them both, nearly tipping them. Niko had swung out on the rope and dive-bombed them. Shrieking, both girls kicked at him as he tried to swim closer. Laughing, Niko shook his dark hair as he treaded water.

"Nice going, jerk!" Allie said as he splashed at her.

"Bitch," Niko said around a long spurt of water.

Jenni laughed, but Allie flipped him the bird. For a second he made as though he was going to swim closer and tip her off the raft; she squealed and kicked at him. He gave up too easily. That was suspicious and meant he'd get Allie back later. The two of them had a competition, kind of but not exactly like the one Jenni had with Ilya. For the briefest second, Jenni looked again at Ilya, then at her sister and finally at Niko, who was swimming back to the shore. Allie and Niko? Nah. That would be too weird.

They floated again in silence, nothing but the wafting tickle of summer songs from the portable radio on the rock outcropping. Jenni didn't know what time it was, but she probably ought to think about heading home to take a shower and get ready for work. She liked the night shifts at the diner because they gave her all day to fuck around, she could sleep in, and the night time was the right time, as the saying went. But not for love, she thought with a small, tight smile that hurt a little like she was twisting her mouth. Night shift at the diner meant truckers who were ready to take it easy for the rest of the night, parked up the road in the spot where they all slept overnight. Truckers who liked the pills Jenni passed them along with their receipts in exchange for the extra large "tips."

She was thinking about Barry again. He'd promised to get her a new supply of the drugs Galina lifted from her job in the surgery unit at the Quarrytown hospital. Good stuff, he'd said. Premium.

"He must have a big dick," Jenni said suddenly.

Allie choked a little. "What? Who? Nikolai? Ew, Jennilynn!"

"No, not Niko. Gawd, Allie, don't be stupid." Jenni used her hands to paddle in the water, turning her in the tube so she could get her head closer to her sister's. She shouldn't even talk about him. She shouldn't mention his name. It was weird of her to do it, she was going to give herself away, but she couldn't help it. "I meant *Barry*."

"Gross, Jenni."

"I bet they screw like rabbits," Jenni said in a tone of secret glee, trying hard to poke her little sis.

Why? It was fun. Again, she knew she shouldn't talk about stuff like that, but it was a compulsion she didn't understand. Imagining Barry fucking Galina. It wasn't like *she* wanted to fuck Barry herself...but she didn't mind knowing that he might want to get in her pants. Married or not, Barry was a guy like they all were. She'd caught him looking at her ass, that fat-not-fat ass. All at once, Jenni's throat closed tight, squeezing, like she was trying not to cry.

Allie grimaced. "Yuck."

Jenni spun, kicking gently. "I bet they do. I bet they do it every night. They're newlyweds, right? Isn't that what they do? I'm going to ask Ilya if he ever hears them. You know his room is right next to theirs."

"Jenni, no. That's..." Allie made a gagging *yuck* sound.

Teasing her sister always chased away the dark thoughts. Laughing, Jenni started to float away, out of Allie's reach. That was when Niko jumped off the rope swing again, this time landing much closer to them. The water swelled, tossing Allie off the raft. Jenni's tube flipped, sending her into the water too.

She'd drawn in a huge breath on instinct as soon as she knew she was going under. Her lips pressed tight, but for a moment, Jenni almost opened her mouth and breathed in, not out. It would be so easy to let the water take her. Wouldn't it?

Something moved in the water between her and Allie. Something orange. Fins tipped with black. It was gone so fast that Jenni couldn't even be sure it had ever been there, but the sight of it had her legs kicking, pushing her up and out of the water. Chester, the carnival goldfish, alive in the quarry? It couldn't be. Jenni laughed, spitting out water.

"Where's Allie?"

Niko had been treading water close to the overturned raft. Jenni's tube had started making its way out toward the center of the water. Jenni spun by kicking and paddling.

"Shit," Niko barked out, "she's still under."

He dove, for a moment his red bathing suit showing above the water's surface. He splashed and resurfaced, hauling Allie with him. She was clearly panicked, almost fighting him, but Niko pulled her with strong, smooth strokes toward the small patch of ground that made up the shore. Out of the water, Allie heaved up a gush of water but didn't puke. She swung and punched Nikolai just below the eye, making him fall back.

"Where's Jenni?" Allie demanded.

"I'm right here. Hey. It's okay. You're okay, right?" Jenni gave Niko a worried look.

Her own fantasies of drowning vanished, faced with the real fact that Allie could have. Her sister fell back onto the dirt and weeds and closed her eyes. She looked so much younger with her wet hair plastered over her face, and Jenni remembered how it had been when they were little. How Allie had followed her around, bugging her all the time. How things had changed over the years. But she still loved her sister, Jenni thought. That wasn't different, even if everything else felt like it was.

"I'm sorry, Allie." Niko sounded anxious. "I was just getting you back for scaring me the other night. Hey, Allie, look at me. I'm sorry."

His apology didn't stop Allie from being pissed off. She sat and tossed her hair out of her eyes. "You're such a giant asshole, Nikolai!"

"I said I was sorry." He grinned.

Jenni looked between the two of them, assessing it. They didn't even see it. Attraction. The tension twirled and tightened, neither Allie or Niko acknowledging it, but Jenni felt it as clearly as if it had been a spiderweb strung with dew that she'd walked into.

Assured her little sis was okay, though, she left the two of them squabbling at the base of the steep slope and made her way up the rocky hill to the rocky outcropping. Theresa had gone, taking her book and towel. Ilya was sitting, his knees pulled to his chest.

"She okay?" he asked.

Jenni nodded and hesitated before sitting next to him on the towel. The rocks were hard under her butt. She and Ilya sat close but not touching. Still, she felt the heat radiating off him. Hotter than the sun.

"I need to leave for work soon," she said.

Ilya lowered his voice, his eyes searching hers. "Let's go back to your house. Your parents won't be home yet."

"Riiiight." She let the word draw out and rolled her eyes. "And what would we do there?"

He shot her a grin. "Whatever we wanted?"

She unfolded herself to stand over him. The sun behind her, her body cast him into shadow. Even so, he shaded his eyes to look up at her.

"I don't think so." It wasn't the answer she wanted to give him, but the last time they'd fooled around, he'd gotten so bent out of shape about it all that it didn't seem worth it.

Anyway, she had a date, of sorts, later tonight, and what was she, some kind of slut? Ilya didn't know about the date, and he wasn't going to. She didn't owe him an explanation about anything. He was just the boy who lived across the street. Just because she loved him, that didn't give him the right to own anything about her.

"Another time?" he asked.

"I don't think so," Jenni repeated.

His face looked like she'd kicked him in the nuts. He'd curse her now. Call her names. Some of them, she might deserve. She braced herself, but Ilya only shrugged and rolled over onto his stomach. Ignoring her.

She watched him for a few seconds, thinking she could change her mind. They could go back to the way things were. They could pretend together, at least for the hour or so they had before she'd have to shove him off her and get in the shower so she could get ready for work. They could pretend life had not moved on.

Except it had.

Chapter 11
TRISTAN

Then

Tristan's father had not been home for the past five days, and for all Tristan knew, would not be home for another five. He always figured that one day his dad simply wouldn't bother coming home at all. That wouldn't be terrible, except that of course Tristan would be left with all the bills for the duplex, but he was already over eighteen and if that happened, he'd just up and head out of town. College wasn't an option at this point, or at least he hadn't bothered to apply to any because there wasn't any money for tuition. But he'd work somewhere. Do something.

It might not be a bad idea to do that anyway, without waiting for Steve Weatherfield to fuck off into the great wide yonder. Tristan would graduate from high school in a few months, and after that he could pack some things and simply…go. Stay with his mom and her new husband for a bit, the way she always claimed she wanted him to. Visit his grandparents in Colorado. He had lots of relatives scattered all over the country, and some of them might be persuaded to let him couch surf for a little while.

The thought of all this put a small grin on his face for the first time all day. The school day had been long and full of suck. He had no plans to see Rebecca tonight, which was the only time he could, because in school they were still both pretending they didn't even know each other's names.

He told himself he liked it that way. Rebecca Segal had money and parents who gave a shit about things all the time, not just every once in a while when it seemed like it might get them something they wanted. She had a future, far away from this town, and Tristan, for all his imaginings only moments before, knew that even if he did pack up and go, his future would never match hers. She wasn't the girl for him, not long term, and if something couldn't last, why should he let himself get all caught up in it now?

A knock at the front door got him off the couch. "Hey, Dereece."

Dereece Washington had lived in the other half of the duplex since before Tristan was born. His wife had died a year ago, and since then he'd been making dinner for Tristan a few times a week. At first, Tristan hadn't wanted to hang out with the old guy, but Dereece had been a professional chef for most of his life, only retiring a couple years back. The dude could cook.

"I made a nice penne pasta with a pesto sauce. Ha, that's almost like a poem." Dereece grinned, showing straight white teeth. "Your dad's not here?"

"Nope."

"More for the two of us, then."

It was kind of a joke. Even when Steve was home, he didn't ever go to eat next door. Tristan's father might not admit aloud he was a racist son-of-a-bitch, but he was. He'd always hated sharing the duplex with the Washingtons, but since he and Tristan's mom had been the ones to buy the other half long after Dereece and Regina had been living there, he had no choice.

Next door, Tristan urged Dereece to sit at the impeccably laid table so he could serve. The older man's arthritis had been bothering him more and more, and it was getting harder for him to lift heavy pots and pans. Tristan would clean the dishes for him later, too. It was worth it, for the food.

"Pour me a little of that red," Dereece said. "Some for you, too, if you want."

Tristan hadn't developed a taste for wine, but he took a small amount. With Dereece, it wasn't about getting drunk. It was about how the wine paired with the food, the entire culinary experience of it. They clinked their glasses. Sipped. Dug in.

"Good pasta," Tristan said.

They didn't talk much while eating. Not in a bad way, like how it was the few nights when Tristan's father was home and at the table with the sports pages and the little betting book he kept next to the phone. A six-pack of beers, dirty dishes, belches and regular complaints about the shit quality of the meal Tristan had put together or they'd ordered for takeout. No, Tristan and Dereece had a comfortable silence, broken by noises of appreciation for the food. Sitting and eating with the older man was more than comfortable. It was *comfort*.

The thought struck him, and his mouth twisted. It was deep, emotional, embarrassing. He looked up to see Dereece giving him a quizzical look.

"You look like something's got you going in there."

Dereece tapped his own temple with a finger, then pointed at Tristan.

"My English teacher was talking about introspection and the inner narrative in school today. I guess I just realized I have an inner narrative." Tristan grinned to cover how awkward it felt to say that out loud.

Dereece chuckled and wiped his mouth with the cloth napkin he insisted on instead of paper. "Don't we all?"

"I don't think so. No." Tristan meant his father. He doubted that guy had an internal anything going on, but if he did, it was probably just a bunch of four letter words and dirty jokes.

"What's your inner narrative saying? Well, I guess if you tell me what it is, it won't be inner, anymore."

"I just was thinking that…" Tristan cleared his throat. Dereece looked expectant. "I like dinners with you. That's all. It's nice to sit and have a good meal with someone at a nice table. And it's okay if we don't talk. It's just nice."

Dereece took a second before nodding. He lifted his wine glass toward Tristan. "Cheers, son."

It wasn't until later, after Tristan had helped the older man clean up his kitchen and then had gone home to his empty, quiet house, that Tristan realized how much it had meant for Dereece to call him that.

He answered his phone on the first ring. "Hey."

"How'd you know it was me?"

Tristan grinned, leaning against the wall in the kitchen, and closed his eyes to imagine her face. "Nobody else would be calling here this time of night."

"It's not too late, is it?" Rebecca asked in a low voice, sort of hesitant.

"No, not too late."

He took the phone upstairs to his bedroom as she told

him about her day. Closed the door, then again when the faulty lock on it allowed it to swing open. Tristan settled himself on the bed, propped on the pillows. Rebecca had been silent for a few seconds.

"What are you doing right now?" she asked.

"Nothing. Talking to you. Thinking about laundry."

She laughed. "What about it?"

"I need to do some."

"You do your own laundry?" She sounded shocked, not impressed.

He furrowed his brow. "Yeah. Don't you?"

"No, the housekeeper does it."

Neither of them spoke for a moment. Then Tristan said, "Do you even know how to do laundry?"

"Of course I do, I mean…sure. Of course." Now she sounded both indignant and embarrassed.

"Want to come over and do mine?"

"You're kidding." She laughed.

God, that laugh. The Rebecca of these late night phone calls was not the Rebecca from school, the one who never even glanced in his direction. She wasn't even the one from the party, made brave by vodka punch. This Rebecca laughed with him, and it was genuine and real and every time he heard the happiness in her voice, Tristan could only think about making sure she always sounded like that.

"Nope. I have a couple loads all ready to go."

"It's almost nine."

"Your parents won't let you out?" He knew the answer to that before she replied.

"No. I mean, I doubt it. They'd at least want to know where I was going."

He shifted on the pillows. "And you can't tell them."

"No."

"Too bad." Tristan lowered his voice. "I really want to see you."

The hitch of her breath was very loud even through the phone line and distance. "Oh."

"Do you want to see me?"

She didn't answer.

"Rebecca," he whispered. "Answer me."

"Yes, Tristan. Yes, I want to see you."

"Let me come over, then." He sat up and swung his legs over the edge of the bed.

"No!"

"I can be there in fifteen minutes."

Her breathing grew faster and harsher before softening. "You can't. I mean, I can't meet you."

"Sneak me into your room."

"Oh my God." She laughed. "You're crazy."

"About you," Tristan said.

Both of them fell silent again. This game had rules neither of them had defined, and it felt like he'd just broken one. He didn't want to take back the words, but he did wonder if she was going to hang up on him.

"Why?" Rebecca's voice was hesitant.

She'd said no, but she might change her mind, so Tristan got up from the bed to gather his keys, wallet, some cash. His shoes. "Why wouldn't I be?"

"That's not an answer."

Tristan grabbed his jacket from the back of the closet door. "I like the way your mouth tastes."

The strangled noise she made gave him pause. The words had whispered out of him without thought. They'd been too much, he thought. Nobody said things like that to each other. Not kids their age, anyway. He'd just laid himself bare in front of her worse than if he'd actually stripped naked.

"Oh my God," she whispered finally.

"Sorry, that was--"

"No, don't be sorry. Oh my God," she repeated. "Yes. Come over."

Chapter 12
JENNI

Then

They'd been making out on the couch in Ilya's living room for hours. Jenni's lips felt puffy and sore. There was an ache in her lower belly and between her legs that she never felt with anyone else. It made her crazy, because it seemed like unless she took his hand and put it down her pants, Ilya was never going to move them along from dry humping to something more satisfying for both of them.

Jenni had lost her virginity a few months ago, and although she would never have admitted that in her fantasies she'd always given it up right here on this couch, with this boy, she also didn't regret the way it had happened. The first time had been as terrible as she'd always been told it would be, but it got better fast after that. She sure as hell wasn't holding on to any lingering guilt or anything about it, the way she knew she was supposed to.

If she shifted beneath him right now, Ilya might at least let her go down on him. They'd done that a couple times.

Never talked about it, after. Both pretended it hadn't happened. He'd never offered to reciprocate, either, but she thought he would if she prompted him to.

That was the issue, wasn't it? That no matter how many times they'd ended up here, Jenni always had to be the one initiating. It was hard enough to find a time when the house was empty, without parents or siblings, so you'd think that the moment they had the place to themselves that he'd have her jeans unzipped before she had a chance to even think about it.

Ilya had muttered something that, too caught up in her sexual frustration, Jenni hadn't heard. "Huh?"

"What if you were my girlfriend? Like. Legit."

Stunned, she laughed aloud. "Us? Dating? Like a real thing?"

"You don't have to make it sound like such a bad thing," Ilya answered, sounding irritated. "Yeah, us. A real thing. Dating."

"Out in public?" She'd snuck in through the back door when everyone else was asleep. This had always been a secret. The idea of taking it public, making it real, shocked her.

She couldn't tell Ilya about Steve, and as much as she fantasized about telling Steve about Ilya to make him jealous, she never would. If she and Ilya made this a real thing, not something secret, she'd have to break off what she had going already. That would be complicated.

Ilya sat back against the couch. "Yeah."

"Don't you like us being like this?"

She reached for him. She didn't want to believe he meant what he'd said, didn't want to give in to the lift her heart had felt at the suggestion. Being with Ilya would feel like…what? A rescue, yet one without safety, because what could be more dangerous than trusting him with her love?

He held himself away. "Look, if we're going to keep doing this in secret, but you won't even let me touch you, and you won't touch me, what's the point, Jenni?"

She got quiet. Her throat closed with tears that also stung her eyes. Is that what he thought? That she wasn't "letting" him touch her? Because now it was clear that all of this was her fault. Ilya blamed her. She was the one who he expected to be guiding this, once again, and she hated him for making her feel like somehow she'd been the one to mess it up. She was a prude if she didn't give it up to him and a whore if she made the first move. There was no winning with boys, not when they became men, either. It disgusted her suddenly. The only reason he wanted her to be his girlfriend was so they'd fuck around, and that pissed her off.

"See, I knew that was all you wanted," she said.

"Of course it's what I want," Ilya snapped with a tug at the crotch of his jeans, making a big show of it. "What guy doesn't want to get laid?"

"But you want me to be your girlfriend?" She shot back, tasting the scorn like scorched toast. "Go on dates? Be a *couple*?"

Ilya frowned. "What's so wrong with that?"

"If all you want is to get laid," Jenni muttered, "why bother with the rest of the bullshit? All that hearts and flowers crap. So, what, you can get your dick sucked on the regular? And after that, what? When you figure out that you're done with me, you can dump me and go get laid by someone else?"

"What's your problem?" Ilya put an arm's length of distance between them. "What, are you on your period?"

Her reply came on a hiss, the words filtering through a sneer so twisted it hurt her face. She should have known better than to think for even one second that Ilya Stern really wanted her to be his girlfriend. To do what? Wear his class ring? Kiss him by the lockers? It was bullshit.

"Oh, right, because a girl gets mad, that means she's on her period. Did it ever occur to you that maybe I'm just tired of all this shit from guys like you?"

"Guys like who?"

"Just...all guys." Jenni flapped her hands at him, shadows upon shadows. "You all want sex and that's it."

Ilya leaned forward to rest his elbows on his knees so he could scrub at his face. "I just told you I wanted to make you my girlfriend, Jenni. Take you out. Make it a real thing, not some kind of secret sex thing. Why do you have to twist it around like that? You're the one making this into that sort of thing. Not me."

"And what happens when you want to break up with me?"

His expression was too hard to see in the shadows. "What makes you think I'd want to?"

Wouldn't he? It might be great at first, especially if they were fucking. But something would happen and he'd be tired of it, of her, or she'd make him angry and he'd decide it wasn't worth putting up with her, not even for a steady supply of blowjobs. He'd make it all her fault, too. Pull her close, push her away, keep her guessing so she doubted her own worth all the fucking time.

"It's what happens," she said in a small and broken voice. "And then what?"

"Jenni..." he reached for her, but she kept herself out of reach, so he stopped reaching.

"It's what happens," she said again, firmly this time. "So we'd have this thing for a little while, and then you break up with me --"

"*You* could break up with me," Ilya retorted.

Jenni swiped at her tears. "Whatever. Then we hate each other."

"How could you think I would ever hate you?" Ilya shook his head.

"Well, it's not like you *love* me," she spat.

Love. That was a huge thing to say out loud, and she'd said it. She could never take it back. Relationships might not last, but love was forever.

Ilya said nothing.

This was worse than when Steve muttered it in her ear when he was on top of her. She never believed Steve meant it, but at least he said it. She could deal with that lie better than this obvious truth. Ilya Stern did not, would never, love Jenni Harrison. Steve would disappoint her but he'd never break her heart, and that was all Ilya would ever do.

"I have to go." Jenni got up. "This is all bullshit, Ilyushka."

He frowned. "Don't call me that."

It was what Babulya called him. A term of endearment. Of love. Jenni had thought of him that way for a long time but had never said it aloud. Now she regretted it.

"Maybe I just won't call you *anything*," Jenni whispered, not moving away. She stood in front of him.

He could have reached for her again. She would have let him touch her, if he had, and if he'd hesitated, she'd have undone the button and zip on her own jeans. Lifted her own shirt. If only he'd reached for her, Jenni would have given herself to Ilya right then and made sure he knew how she felt.

Ilya did not reach for her. Without another word, Jenni left him there. In the kitchen, a silhouette startled her. Galina's husband, Barry.

"You scared the shit out of me," Jenni hissed at him. "Jesus Christ."

"Everything okay?" Glass glinted off the vodka bottle Barry was using to fill his shot glass.

Jenni frowned. "Peachy."

"Sounded like you were having a fight."

"None of your business," she told him.

"I make your business mine, Jennilynn. Want to make sure you're all right. Need my best girl at her best." Barry was slurring. In the dark, his smile flashed.

Jenni's skin crawled. Barry had never made a weird move on her or anything like that, but he was still kind of a creep. She knew Ilya didn't like him. Ilya would fucking hate him if he knew the truth about everything that Barry and Galina were into and what they'd both convinced Jenni to do for them.

She didn't bother answering him. He was drunk enough that it wouldn't matter, anyway. She went out the back door and across the crumbling concrete patio, through the overlong grass and to the street.

Her parents would wake up if tried to pull the car out of the garage, but the thought of going home made her stomach churn. If Allie woke up when she climbed in the window, little sis would want to know where Jenni had been. Instead, Jenni went to the path leading into the woods.

In the equipment shed, she dug through the litter in the corner to find the mason jar in which she'd put the mint tin that held the supply of pills she was supposed to sell. Keeping it at home had become too risky. She shook the tin and lifted it to the shaft of moonlight, but decided it didn't matter which one she took. All of them were going to do something to her that would make her feel better, at least for a little while.

She dry swallowed one and put the tin back. She made her way through the rest of the path, to the place where they'd hung the rope swing. Now on unsteady feet, the world hazy and swirling around her, she managed to get herself to the rocky outcropping that overlooked the water. She sat there with her legs hanging over the edge. The pill made her just loopy enough that when she found herself swaying forward, almost losing her balance, she wasn't even scared.

Jenni looked down into the black water below. How many hours had they spent here, swimming and sunning themselves? Summer seemed so long ago. She wished it were summer right now.

She wouldn't be here next summer. She knew that as clearly as she knew her own name. By then, no matter how she had to make it happen, Jenni would be gone from Quarrytown.

Gone for good.

Chapter 13
REBECCA

Then

Rebecca's parents had gone to bed an hour or so before, but the house was not yet quiet. The low hum of the television sometimes wafted toward her. They were still awake.

Tristan would be here any minute. Thinking of it, her stomach twisted and churned. She'd taken a shower and combed through her wet hair, letting the dark curls air dry. She smoothed her body with scented lotion but didn't add perfume. It wasn't like she wanted him to think she was making a huge effort.

Right?

She pushed open her window a crack, letting in a gust of frigid air. Bending low, she shielded her eyes to look out to the street, searching for a glimpse of headlights. With the lights on inside her room, the glass was too reflective. Her reflection, a little warped, set her back a step.

They'd been doing this thing for a few months now. They'd talk on the phone. They'd meet at the movies in the next town over. Park in the dark shadows of parking lots for closed shops. A few weeks ago, he'd asked to come over and they'd been doing that ever since.

She'd always say yes, but never make the initial invitation. The game, and that's for sure what it was, a stupid game they both seemed to like to play, had only one real rule. All of this stayed a secret.

Tristan never asked Rebecca if she was breaking up with Richie. To be honest, in her head, she wasn't with Richie any more, even if they hadn't had an outright discussion about it. They hardly ever spoke on the phone. They didn't sit together at lunch — he stuck with his friends and she with hers. They hadn't even gone out together for more than three weeks. Richie hadn't asked her, and Rebecca hadn't asked him, and even if they hadn't officially broken up, she told herself, how could he possibly think that they were still together if they never saw each other?

It was a justification, and she knew it. Still, Rebecca had convinced herself that if the subject did come up, she'd tell Richie the truth. Well, not the whole truth. Nothing about Tristan. But yeah, she'd tell Richie it would be best if they broke up. If he asked her, she'd say so.

She'd almost given up on Tristan by the time the soft rap sounded at her window. Irritated at being made to wait but more annoyed at how anxious it had made her to think he wasn't going to make it, Rebecca pushed the window up all the way so he could climb inside. He landed with a thump, too loud, and she shushed him.

"I didn't think you were coming," she said.

Tristan shrugged, not meeting her gaze. "My next door neighbor was sick. I had to help him out."

Now she felt like exactly the sort of bitch she knew some people thought she was. "Is he okay?"

Tristan shook his head, but said nothing more.

"I'm sorry," Rebecca said.

This was definitely not the normal vibe between them. Tristan normally came in through the window with a grin, flirting right away. Tonight he paced for a minute before stopping in front of her bookcase. The shelves held her collection of music boxes, most of them ballerina themed. She'd stopped collecting years ago, except for every Chanukah when her mother presented her with a new one.

"Are you a dancer?" Tristan touched one of the tiny ballerinas, urging her to spin out a few disjointed notes.

"No. My mom always wanted me to take ballet, but I never liked it. She started the collection for me when she was pregnant. She buys me a new one every year," Rebecca added. "I wish she'd stop."

Tristan looked over his shoulder, then turned to face her. "Why not just tell her?"

"It would hurt her feelings."

"Maybe it would hurt her feelings more if you never told her how you felt, and she just kept going on and on, doing something she thought you liked, but you don't."

She frowned.

"Maybe," Tristan continued when she didn't say anything, "you should just tell your mom how you really feel instead of letting her feel kind of like an asshole."

Rebecca blinked. "I don't make my mom feel like an asshole!"

"You sure?"

"I…" She lifted her chin and crossed her arms. "That's a shitty thing to say."

Neither of them spoke for a moment. Tristan sighed and rubbed at his eyes, turning from her to look again at the shelf of music boxes. He tapped another one, but it didn't make a sound.

"You don't have any books," he said.

Again, she blinked, this time at his tone. "Huh?"

"You don't have any books. You don't read?"

"I read," Rebecca said, insulted.

It was true, though. She didn't have any books other than the ones she needed for school. It had never occurred to her before this moment that something would be wrong with that. The look on Tristan's face, a mixture of disappointment and disdain, embarrassed her.

"Maybe you should just leave," she told him.

He looked toward the window. Then her. His shoulders slumped, his expression crestfallen and low. "I'm worried about my neighbor."

To her surprise and also her concern, he drew in a hitching breath and sat heavily on her bed. He put his face in his hands. This was not the Tristan she was used to. Uncertain, Rebecca sat beside him and put a tentative arm around his shoulders.

"He's lost a lot of weight. I think he's got something bad, like cancer, only he won't say." Tristan's breath shuddered. He didn't look at her.

Still not sure what to do for him, Rebecca tugged him down onto her bed, turning them both so she could spoon him. Her arms around him, her chin on his shoulder. She listened to his breathing smooth. She slipped her hand up to his chest, feeling the thrum and beat of his heart, too fast at first, until it also settled.

"He's a good old guy. He lost his wife a few years ago. He had a son, but I think he died, too. He never talks about him, but there was a picture on the mantel. Young kid in an army uniform." Tristan's voice, low and shaky, cut off.

He was crying. She didn't know what to do or say to him. So she said nothing and only held him. When he turned on the bed to bury his face against her, Rebecca ran her fingers through his hair, over and over again, until he stopped shaking.

"I don't want him to die," Tristan whispered into the base of her throat.

"I'm sorry," she said.

He held her tight, but said nothing else. Eventually, the steady in-out of his breathing told her that he slept. Carefully, Rebecca pulled away to turn out the bedside light. In the dark, she gathered him close to her again. She breathed in time with him. If she dreamed, she didn't remember it, and when she woke to the absence of him in her arms, she wondered if he'd ever been there at all.

Chapter 14
JENNI

Then

The Sterns and the Harrisons had been in the habit of moving back and forth between the only two houses there at the end of Quarry Street, so Jenni wasn't shocked when Niko showed up and let himself into the house. He tossed her one of the cookies in his fist.

Jenni caught it, barely managing not to crumble it although she was in the middle of painting her nails. She ate it anyway, because she wasn't about to pass up one of Babulya's cookies. She eyed the daytime soap she'd been watching.

"Jerk, you made me mess up my polish."

"Bitch," Niko said.

It was the standard comeback they all used, not an insult. Jenni rolled her eyes. "Where's your brother?"

She regretted asking the moment the words slipped out of her mouth. If she'd been suspecting that Niko and Allie were harboring sexy feelings for each other, it could be reasonable to think that Niko might suspect the same of her and his brother. She didn't want anyone to know it, but especially not Niko, who would certainly tell Allie. Allie would then pester Jenni about it, and what would Jenni be able to tell her? Nothing. She would never be able to say a word.

Niko shrugged. "I think he went over to Kim Lee's house."

Jenni flinched. Kim Lee had been crushing on Ilya since seventh grade. She was always trying to spread rumors about Jenni. Nobody ever believed them, because Kim Lee was known to be a big fat liar. If Ilya was fooling around with her, Jenni might literally puke.

Niko flopped onto the couch beside her and propped his feet on the coffee table, but first snagged the remote to change the station. He laughed at her cry of protest and held the remote up and out of her reach.

"Jerk," Jenni muttered again, then fixed him with a steady look. He'd thrown Kim Lee in her face. She could do a little of the same. "Allie isn't home, by the way. She stayed after to do something for the play."

Niko looked caught. So he did *like* Allie. He gave an exaggerated shrug and turned toward the TV screen. "Why do you think that matters to me?"

The pager on Jenni's hip beeped and she grabbed for it with a small, secret grin, studying the number on the small black screen. It was code, one of the dozens of strings of numbers that meant full phrases. She held the pager to her chest for a moment. Did a little seated dance. Steve. She hadn't heard from him for a couple weeks. He never contacted her when he was on the road.

I want to fuck you.

Niko strained to catch a look at the pager. "Got a boyfriend or something?"

"None of your business, buttstain," Jenni said, but she

was distracted. Paying too much attention to the message on the pager to notice that Niko was close enough to snag it from her grip.

"Give me that, shithead!" Jenni swept the pager out of his hand and punched him on the arm for good measure.

"Sorry," he muttered. "You don't have to be such a bitch about it."

"Fuck you, Niko." Her heart pounded. Had he seen the message? Even if he had, it wasn't any of his business. He had no idea who it had come from. Her stomach churned, twisting at the idea of being caught.

Without another word, Niko got off the couch and left the room. Jenni stared after him. He'd definitely seen the message and interpreted it. He might tell Ilya. Well, that wouldn't matter. If Ilya asked her about it, she didn't have to tell him anything about it. Or she could tell him everything.

Swiftly, she typed in the code 6-9999999 — *get in line.*

Breathless, she waited to see what he'd reply. It felt empowering, this flirting. The back and forth. Being pursued. It was a recent development, his chase. The tables were turning, and although Jenni didn't know exactly why or how it had happened, she liked it.

In the beginning, serving him coffee and sometimes a few small white or blue pills passed along with the check, Jenni had flirted with Steve the way she flirted with all the customers. A bright smile, a toss of her hair. Sometimes, she'd lean over a little too far when pouring the coffee, and even though she never let her tits hang out of her waitress uniform, the men never, ever failed to try and look down the front of her dress. Men were predictable. She'd learned that right away.

Steve hadn't been so predictable. Dark hair. Dark eyes. The scruff of a dark beard feathered with silver. He hadn't smiled or tried to joke with her. He'd simply, one night, jerked his head toward the parking lot and described his truck.

She hadn't gone with him that night, but two weeks later, after he'd "tipped" her enough to get a couple pills from her supply, she had gone out after work to see him standing next to the big rig. Smoking a cigarette. Waiting for her? She'd thought so, but wasn't sure. She'd climbed inside the cab of his truck and let him kiss her. Let him do more than that, too.

He wasn't like the other truckers who came to the diner, because Steve was a local. His truck was only ever in the lot on his way out of town, or maybe on his way back in. Sometimes, he showed up at the diner in his black Camaro. Sometimes, he even took her for a drive in it. But the only times they ever fucked around were in the cab of his truck.

Jenni never asked why Steve didn't take her home. She wasn't sure she'd have gone with him, if he'd asked. Doing it this way kept it in a certain place, made it a certain type of thing. Only now, Steve was making more of this whatever-it-was.

345987 — I'm horny

She rolled her eyes.

335, she typed. *You're crazy.*

She was the crazy one, though. Playing with fire. He'd already put his hands on her, too hard, too much, when once she'd refused to go down on him. He'd been sorry after, or said he was, but the truth was that she hadn't minded. When she was alone, Jenni looked at the bruises he left and felt her heart pound. They were proof of... something. She didn't quite understand what or why, but something big, vast, beyond her.

"I want out of this place," she'd told him the last time they'd been together.

"So," Steve had said, "let's get the fuck out of here."

Maybe tonight she'd take the roll of cash she'd been saving, put it in her pocket. Leave everything else behind. She'd get in Steve's truck with him and get out of here, just like he said.

Maybe.

Chapter 15
JENNI

Then

It was so cold, Jenni could see her breath. Looking at the stars overhead, she wondered if it would be worth making a wish. She wished Ilya had sat next to her at the battered picnic table in the Stern back yard, the way Allie and Niko were sitting. Instead Jenni and Ilya sat as far apart from each other as they could get.

He hated her, or he wanted her to think he did. Well, sometimes she hated him, too, even though she loved him. Jenni couldn't remember when she'd stopped thinking of him as just the boy who lived across the street. It would have been so much easier if she'd never started thinking of him as anything else.

Only two days ago, she'd come over here in the afternoon. Both Barry and Galina's cars were gone. She'd found Ilya in his room, jamming to music while he flipped through a sports magazine. She'd wanted to see if he would kiss her. Touch her. She wanted, maybe to get him to go all the way with her, kind of like a test.

She wanted a reason not to run away from here, but Ilya hadn't given her one. They'd fought, instead. He'd been cold and derisive. She'd been shrill. They'd ended up saying things that still left a bad taste in her mouth. He blamed her, she knew, for being what he thought was a tease.

"How long do we have to wait? It's freaking cold out here." Ilya shrugged deeper into his heavy winter coat and acted like he wasn't eyeing Jenni from the corner of his eye.

He should've just sat next to her. He wanted to. Jenni wanted him to. Too bad neither of them would admit it. They both were freezing their asses off. Not for the first time, she longed for the days when they'd been just friends, before the tension between them and the promise of something more had changed everything. She and Ilya had known each other forever, but now she didn't feel like she knew him at all.

"It might be too cloudy." Niko stretched out his legs and leaned his head back to look up into the winter sky.

"Just watch," Jenni said. "It's going to be amazing."

Tonight, something special was supposed to happen. An alignment of the planets, nine of them. Something rare. A once-in-a-lifetime event, the sort of thing you wanted to share with the people you love best in all the world. That was the four of them, together, the way they'd been for so long. Friends. More than friends. Family. Lovers.

Allie rested her head on Niko's shoulder and smiled when he tilted his to rest on hers. Beneath the blanket covering them both, they thought nobody would see they were holding hands. A horrible pang of envy sliced through Jenni, worse than a razor. Allie and Niko? It should have been Jenni and Ilya, too, but it would never be.

"Wouldn't it be great," Niko said, "If we could travel into space the way we can fly in an airplane?"

Ilya inched closer to Allie's side to grab some of the blanket, and as if on cue, she and Niko both pulled their hands from underneath it. "Why would you want to?"

"I'd like to," Jenni said. She did not move closer to Niko's other side, although the blanket was big enough for all of them. "Just...fly away."

Ilya leaned to look at her. "Where would you go?"

"Anywhere."

"I'm with you," Niko said. "Get out of this town. See something. Do something important."

He got it. He understood. It was his older brother who seemed stuck here, determined to live his whole life within the confines of Quarrytown.

"It's not happening," Ilya said impatiently with a gesture at the sky. "Or if it is, we aren't going to be able to see it with these clouds."

"Patience," Niko said, and Jenni and Allie both laughed, because Ilya didn't have any.

"I'll be right back." Jenni scooted off the picnic table. "I have to go to the bathroom."

"Refill the thermos," Allie suggested and handed it to her sister.

Jenni took it. Inside the Sterns' kitchen, she set the thermos on the counter and put the kettle on to boil the water while she used the toilet. When she came back out, Barry's dark silhouette leaned in the doorway.

"I'm due a deposit," he said.

"I don't have it with me." Jenni didn't look at him.

She hadn't given Barry anything for two weeks, and the last time she had, it had been lighter than it should have been. She'd said it was because nobody was buying, or if they were, they were haggling about the pricing. It was a lie. She was taking a cut and holding it back. She deserved it though, didn't she? She was the one taking the risk by making the sales.

"You haven't been holding out on me, have you?" His tone was light, but the words were menacing.

Jenni helped herself to the container of hot cocoa mix in the cupboard, too aware of Barry's gaze on her as she moved about the kitchen in the house that wasn't hers. She poured powder into the thermos. The kettle wasn't crying yet.

"No. Of course not," she lied.

"Avoiding me, though, aren't you?"

She faced him finally. "No. I've just been busy. I'm in high school and I have a job and —"

"A boyfriend," Barry put in. "Right?"

"I don't have a boyfriend," Jenni muttered.

"You have someone."

Jenni shook her head, mute. What she had was not up for conversation, especially not with fucking *Barry*. Still, the fact he knew, or only suspected, gave her pause.

"My life isn't any of your business," she said.

A clicking noise issued from Barry's throat. "I need to move product, Jennilynn. More of it. The supplies do me no good if you can't get it into the hands of the people who want it."

"I've been busy at school. I haven't had as many shifts at the diner. That's all."

"I'd hate to think you were maybe just trying to go around me or something. Or maybe you were skimming?" Barry moved a step closer.

Jenni held up a hand. "Don't you fucking dare, Barry. I will scream so fucking loud."

"Not sure what you thought I was going to do to you," he said but kept his distance. Incredibly, he sounded a little hurt that she would even suggest he might have tried something inappropriate.

"You don't scare me."

Barry laughed. "Look, I'm not trying to scare you."

"Then don't make stupid fake threats," she told him in a low, furious tone. "Because guess what, you and I both know that if anyone finds out about any of this, you're the one who's going to get in the worst trouble. You and Galina. Not me!"

"Nobody's going to get in trouble." Now he was trying to placate her.

The kettle began to scream, and Jenni yanked it off the burner. She blinked away the threat of angry tears. She filled the thermos with boiling water and put on the lid, then shook it to mix the cocoa.

"You're going to burn your mouths on that, if you're not careful," Barry said.

Jenni put the thermos on the counter. "What if I did want to get out of it, huh? What would you do about it? You have a guy ready to rough me up, or what?"

Barry grimaced. "The way you like it, right?"

She went cold, colder than she'd been outside. Frigid down to her toes. "What?"

"You left quite an impression on Dillon."

Before she could stop herself, Jenni touched her throat. The place Steve liked to choke her and she liked him to do it. Quickly, she took her hand away, but Barry had seen her. She wanted to slap his smug grin right off his face.

"Dillon can eat an unsalted barrel of dicks," Jenni said. She hadn't seen him in months. After the night of the party, he'd stopped buying from her and coming around the diner at all. "Does he say we're together?"

"No. Just that you used to be."

Jenni grimaced. "He shouldn't run his mouth."

"Just get me the cash or the pills," Barry said. "One or the other. Then we're golden. If you can't do that, I'll have to find someone else to sell for me."

No. She didn't want that. She wanted the money. And the danger. She needed both.

"You'll get it," she said.

Chapter 16
JENNI

Then

If her parents knew how many times Jenni had climbed up and down this tree to sneak out of the house, her father would have cut it down years ago. Every time she did, she couldn't help thinking about that movie, *Pollyanna*, where the girl fell out of the tree. The fall had messed that kid up bad, but it was just a movie. This was real life.

Jenni slid open the window and swung a leg over the sill. She'd expected to see her sister getting ready for school, but Allie must've been in the shower. Thank God. Jenni didn't have the energy for a fight. Not this morning.

She put a hand over her mouth to fight back the retch that threatened, and looked desperately for something to puke into. There was nothing, and she managed to keep herself from vomiting only because she didn't have any food in her stomach to come up.

She and Steve had spent the night drinking and smoking and getting it on. It had been weeks since the last time he'd paged her, so long she was sure he wasn't going to. They'd fought about it in the cab of his truck. She wasn't his girlfriend, he'd reminded her, and she'd tossed back that *he* wasn't her boyfriend. He'd put his hands on her, hard, and she'd purred like a kitten. It was a fucking mess, one she didn't know how to get out of. One she didn't want to get out of.

Jenni was in bed and settled beneath her faded quilt made from squares her mom had sewn out of old baby clothes and blankies when Allie got back into the bedroom. She'd pulled the covers up over her head and was breathing slowly in and out through her nose to get her stomach to ease. Her eyes felt like someone had ground glass and sprinkled it into them. They were closed, and she swore she could still see swirling bands of color every time she shifted her gaze. She totally got why people took pills, but she wasn't sure she'd ever understand how they could function at all, ever, while doing it.

Allie sounded pissed. "Hey. Get up. You're going to be late for school."

"I'm sick."

"You're *not* sick. You're *hungover*."

"Not." Jenni didn't so much as twitch back the covers. She didn't want to look at her sister. More importantly, she didn't want to have to look at the light.

Allie tried to pull on the blanket, but Jenni had a death grip on it from underneath. They struggled for a few seconds before Allie won. The blankets ripped back. Jenni grimaced and tried to shield her eyes.

"Shit," Allie said, stepping back. "What happened to you?"

"Nothing." It was no use resisting. Jenni sat up, clutching the blankets to her chest.

There were leaves in her hair. Shit. How did she get

leaves in her hair? They'd been in his truck the whole night. Hadn't they?

A vague memory of laughing and stumbling through the dark with trees slapping at her face rose. She'd gone out to the old shed in the woods, the one that had once been used to store equipment when the quarry had been in use. That was where she and Barry met up to exchange pills for dollar bills. She could only remember swallowing a few from the supply she'd brought with her to work. Had Steve urged her to go get more? Another memory swam up from the depths of her mind, even less firm, of Steve driving them to the end of Quarry Street farthest away from her house, of her feet dangling from the high cab as she dropped to the asphalt. He must have sent her to get them more drugs. Damn it, Jenni thought. He'd scammed her.

"You look like crap," Allie said. "What happened to you? Jenni, what happened to your neck?"

Jenni touched her throat and felt a small but angry red scratch just below her chin. She pulled the blankets up higher, hiding herself from view. "It's just a hickey or two."

"Gross. Mom will kill you --"

At the words, Jenni let out a low, snorting laugh that cut off, strangled. "She won't. Kill me. She wouldn't actually *kill* me."

I could kill you, and nobody would figure it out.

The pressure of fingers around her throat, squeezing. Pleasure, rising along with the pain. The haze of drugs and alcohol, his voice in her ear, his hands on her.

I could kill you, if I wanted to, and you'd love it the entire time.

Allie grabbed panties and a bra from the dresser and slipped into them with her back turned, self-conscious in front of her sister, in a way that Jenni had never understood. They had the same parts. They were sisters. But

Allie had always been shy about showing her body. It was good though, for her to turn away. It meant she wasn't staring at Jenni anymore.

"It's just a saying." Allie pulled on a pair of jeans and one of her favorite t-shirts. "And if she or Dad see those hickies all over your neck, you'll be in such bad trouble you'll maybe wish they'd kill you, instead."

"I would never *wish* to be dead."

It was a lie. Jenni wished to be dead almost all the time. It used to be she'd wonder what people would say about her. How they'd gather for a funeral. How'd they all talk about her, so sad, missing her.

She didn't care about any of that anymore. Now, she thought about the long quiet darkness that would accompany death. She imagined it was like sleeping without dreams, not having to wake up, ever again.

Allie whirled around, frowning. "What?"

"Nothing. Never mind. Forget it, you're right, I'm hungover. Shit, maybe still drunk." Jenni mumbled her answer, words slurring a little, and cut her gaze from her sister's. It was the truth. The room was starting to spin again. She dove beneath the blankets again. "Leave me alone now. Tell Mom I'm sick, please? She'll believe you."

Allie was quiet for a second. "Where were you last night?"

"Out in the woods." Also the truth, although nowhere close to all of it.

"Yeah. I can tell. With who. A boyfriend?"

God. That word again, that thing, that stupid term that meant nothing. Jenni was eighteen. Steve was an adult. He probably had "girlfriends" all along his route. She didn't care. What they did wasn't about dating or love. Still, there'd been those times in the darkness of his cab's bed section that he'd buried himself against her and whispered sweet words she'd almost let herself believe, if only because he sounded like he did. If nothing else, he might be the one to give her a ride when she was ready to get out of here. What might happen beyond that wasn't anything she could think about, especially not right now.

Jenni giggled, surprising herself with the humor. "What if I was?"

"Since when do you have a boyfriend?" Allie asked.

"I didn't *say* he was a boyfriend."

Alicia turned, a pair of knee-socks in hand. "You're out with him often enough, whoever it is. Just tell me, Jenni, who is it? Is it someone I know?"

Jenni was silent beneath the blankets for a moment, before she mumbled the lie, "yes. You know him."

It was possible Allie would recognize him. He was at the diner a lot. But Jenni knew for a fact her sister didn't know anything about him. Hell, Jenni didn't even know Steve's last name, herself. Jenni lied because she wanted her sister to think she'd been sneaking out to fool around in the woods with a boy from school.

"Ilya."

"Who? What about Ilya?" Jenni flipped the blanket back, startled and disgruntled that Allie could even say such a thing.

"He's your boyfriend?"

"Why? Did he say he was?" Jenni felt weirdly hopeful, but it lasted only a couple seconds. She and Ilya had gone around and around. He was never going to be what she needed. She would only ever be something he *wanted*. She pulled the blanket back over her face. "Was he talking about me?"

"I haven't asked him. I asked you. If it's not Ilya...who is it?"

Jenni faked a soft snore. Allie didn't ask again. After a

moment, Jenni heard the click of the door closing behind her sister. She waited for her mother to come up and demand she get out of bed, but Allie must have done Jenni a solid and told their mom she really was sick. Jenni would owe her, she supposed. That was okay.

She slept restlessly and woke feeling like shit. She stumbled to the bathroom and ran the shower. She bent over the sink, meaning to brush her teeth while she waited for the water to heat. The sight of her face in the mirror startled a low cry out of her.

Bruises, small but distinct, ringed her throat. Allie was right. They did look gross. They did not look like hickies… because they weren't. Jenni's knees sagged, and she gripped the edges of the sink to keep herself from falling.

She should go to her parents, to the police. She should never let him touch her again. What was wrong with her? Why did she let him do these things to her, over and over, getting worse and worse?

Why did she like it?

Jenni climbed into the shower and tipped up her face into the water. It stung the scratches on her neck. More bruises dotted her body. Her knees, one hip. Those had been from stumbling, high and drunk, through the trees. But there was another pattern of bruises on her breasts, and one nipple had been abraded. She didn't remember what had happened.

She pushed a hand between her legs, unsure what she was feeling for. She found only her own body, no pain, no evidence of anything bad. That meant nothing, but the chances they'd used a rubber were pretty fucking small. She put both her hands flat on her belly, imagining it getting round with a trucker's bastard. Shit, shit, shit.

No. She wasn't pregnant. She couldn't be. She had too

much to do, too many places to go and see. She wasn't knocked up. She was fine.

Shaking, she washed herself. By the time the water had started running cold, Jenni felt a little better, at least until she got back into her room and looked again at her naked body in the mirror. Why the hell had they been in the woods last night? Why had she taken him to the old equipment shed?

Another wave of sickness washed over her. Vaguely, she remembered the pressure of Steve's fingers on her throat. She'd given him all the money she had saved. He promised to keep it safer for her than it would be buried in a jar in the dirt floor of the shed. At the time, it had seemed like that made sense. Now, sober, she realized she'd been the stupid bitch who'd given up everything she had to a man she didn't trust.

Chapter 17
TRISTAN

Then

"Where the fuck've you been?"

At the sound of his father's growl, Tristan jumped back, knocking against the empty beer bottles on the edge of the kitchen counter. One fell onto the linoleum and bounced, without breaking, off his foot. He muttered a curse and hopped on the other foot.

"Watch your mouth," his father said from his seat at the table.

"What are you doing here?" Tristan demanded.

Steve, sitting at the kitchen table with a bottle of beer in front of him, looked like seven kinds of hammered shit. His dark hair, lank with filth, pushed off his forehead to show red-rimmed eyes and a bleary gaze. White froth had curdled and dried in the corners of his mouth. His fingernails, black with grime, drummed the tabletop.

"I live here. I asked you a question."

Tristan kept a wary distance from his father. Steve had never hit him, but there was always a first time. Tristan was sure he could take his dad in a fight, but he didn't want to find out. "I was out."

"You fucking little smart-ass." Steve's lip twitched. "Getting some, huh?"

"Something like that." Tristan was not about to tell his father the truth about anything.

He opened the fridge and pulled out a carton of orange juice and a loaf of bread. He had just enough time to shower and have something to eat before it was time to head to school, where he and Rebecca would pretend they hadn't spent the night together in her bed. He'd been sneaking into her room for weeks.

Thinking of it now, a slow, rolling surge of desire filled him. Not just for the fooling around, all the things they did that were not actual sex but might as well have been. But for all of it. The way she sounded when she slept, the touch of her feet to his under the covers. Shaking it off, Tristan put two slices of cheap white bread in the toaster and punched down the lever.

"I didn't think you'd be home," he said over his shoulder, then glanced at his father when Steve didn't answer right away.

Steve's head was drooping. Jesus, he was sloshed. Or stoned, Tristan realized after a second. The guy was fucking wasted.

"What happened to you?" Tristan asked.

His father blinked and managed to look up at him. "Huh?"

"Your hands are filthy. Were you...gardening, or some shit?"

Of course Steve hadn't been gardening. He couldn't be bothered to mow the lawn or anything like that. The dirt on his hands bothered Tristan because it was so out of place. Grease and oil from working on the engine of his car and sometimes, the big rig? Sure. But soil? Earth? That was shady.

Steve mumbled something that Tristan couldn't quite catch. His head bobbed again. The beer bottle tipped, but it was empty and nothing spilled out. The toast popped up, and Tristan put it on a plate. He crunched it dry, since they were out of butter, jelly or anything else. He watched his father sleep. Steve was going to wake up with a stiff neck, if he didn't fall off the chair entirely and end up on the floor.

Tristan sighed and put the plate of toast on the counter. He crossed to his father and tried lifting him. "C'mon, Dad. Let's get you to bed."

There was no way he was going to get his father up the stairs to bed. The couch would have to do. Tristan didn't bother trying to shove a pillow under Steve's head or anything, but he did take the old man's shoes off. As he stood, Steve shifted and a wad of bills that had been peeking out of his pocket fell out and scattered on the floor.

Tristan paused. He looked to see if Steve was awake. Nope. Tristan picked up the money, tucking it all together. A quick count showed it was nearly all in twenties. A little over a thousand dollars. Why the hell was his dad carrying around a wad of cash?

It took Tristan only a few seconds to run upstairs and pull out the loose board in the back of his closet. He tucked the money away there with the rest of his scant savings, earned from odd jobs and the occasional pilfering he did from Steve's wallet when the guy was drunk. He'd never found so much money before. Steve would probably accuse him of taking it when he got sober, but there was no way he could ever prove it, and Tristan had zero problems lying to his father about anything, especially cash he'd stolen from him. Dereece would have been disappointed in him, Tristan thought with a pang of guilt that passed quickly as he shoved away the following surge of concern about the old man. Dereece would be home from the hospital soon, Tristan told himself. He'd be fine.

Fifteen minutes later he was showered and out of the house, leaving his dad still snoring on the couch. He made it to school a few minutes before the homeroom bell rang. Tristan went to his locker to grab his trig book, the money still on his mind. A brief fantasy of using it to impress Rebecca by taking her out for a fancy dinner, flowers, a movie, the works, crossed his mind. He shoved that thought away fast, the way he did whenever his stupid-ass brain tried to get him thinking of her that way. He needed that money to save in case he ever did decide to leave town.

"…I don't know where she was, so stop fucking asking me!"

The angry voice perked Tristan's ears. It was Ilya Stern, who had the locker a few down from his. Without making it too obvious, Tristan glanced toward the other guy. He was deep in furious conversation with Allie Harrison.

"She looked like someone had beaten her up." Allie said this in a low, miserable voice as she swiped at her eyes. "She wasn't with you? Are you sure?"

Ilya slammed his locker shut. "You think if I'd been with her, I wouldn't tell you? She was out with whoever she's fucking around with, Allie. And whoever that is, it ain't me."

"She was filthy. Like she'd been grubbing around in the dirt! Something's going on with her!"

Tristan twitched, thinking of the dirt grimed under Steve's nails, and involuntarily turned. Ilya caught sight of his staring. The other guy made a threatening gesture.

"The fuck you looking at?"

"Nothing," Tristan said and closed his locker.

It wasn't any of his business, had nothing to do with him, and probably had nothing to do with Steve, either. He looked carefully away from Ilya, not wanting to goad the bigger guy into a fight. He'd never had a problem with Ilya, but that didn't mean he wanted to start one today.

Ilya stormed off, leaving Allie behind. She slumped against the lockers. She didn't weep outright, but she looked miserable.

"Hey, are you okay?" Tristan didn't want to get involved, but it seemed shitty of him to be standing right there and not even ask.

She was in his arms a second after that, her face buried against him. He put his arms around her instinctively, if awkwardly. The embrace lasted only a few seconds before they both pulled away. She looked mortified.

"Sorry, oh my God, I'm sorry."

"It's fine," he said.

Shaking her head, Allie pushed away from him and headed for the girl's bathroom, leaving Tristan to stare after her in confusion. With a shrug, he turned to go to homeroom before the bell rang. The crowd had thinned with kids rushing to get into class before the bell, and there she was, on the other side of the hall.

Rebecca.

Her stare lingered, her expression blank except for the faintest hint of surprise and something else in her gaze. Anger, disappointment, sadness. It was gone in a blink, and she turned and went through the door behind her.

Chapter 18
JENNI

Then

Jenni hadn't said more than a couple words to Ilya in two weeks. He tried to act like he didn't give a shit and a half about what she did or who she did it with, but she knew he'd been going crazy from the silent treatment. Good, she thought with some bitterness. Let him go fucking crazy about it. Let him see he wasn't her only option. Let him suffer.

That she was suffering too, and from her own choices, sent more self-loathing through her that she shoved away. Ilya Stern was not the love of her life. He was the boy across the street, and she wasn't going to stick around this shitty little town just to see if they ended up getting married and making babies and living a shitty little small town life together. She was getting out of here, leaving everyone and everything behind. Yeah, it hurt, but nothing good came without sacrifice.

Right?

Jenni moved from table to table, refreshing coffee and

taking orders. Ilya was sitting in a back booth, acting like he didn't see her. She ignored him. If he really thought she didn't know he was there, he was more of a dumbass than she'd ever thought. For a moment she let herself stare across the room at him but looked away before he could catch her.

Love was nothing but a prison sentence. She loved Ilya because they'd known each other for so long that loving him seemed like her only choice. She loved him because he was there. Because he was cute. Because, because, because.

Because he knew her, and he loved her anyway.

Jenni bit down hard on the inside of her cheek to stop herself from thinking about this. Chin up. Shoulders straight. Ignore the pain inside, ignore everything but her single-focused desire to finish her shift and distribute all the product Barry had given her. Get the money. Get enough.

And then…she'd be gone.

"You have a table that's been waiting," Marie, one of the older waitresses who'd been here forever, said with a gesture toward Ilya's booth. "I asked if I could help him, but he said he'd wait for you. Boyfriend?"

"Not even."

"I could take it over, if you want."

"I'll do it," Jenni said.

Marie touched her on the arm so Jenni looked at her. "You okay, hon? No offense, but you look kinda rough. Like you've lost weight."

Jenni caught a glimpse of her reflection in the diner's mirrored wall. Faint dark circles under her eyes. Her cheeks were more hollow, but since when had being skinny ever been a bad thing? "Can't be too thin, right?"

"Yeah, I guess so." Marie didn't look convinced.

"Just a little tired. I'm fine. I'll get him after I use the bathroom." In the stall, she pulled a couple of pills from her pocket and slipped them into her mouth to dry swallow them.

Jenni closed her eyes, waiting for the flood of numbness. It took hardly any time at all, probably because what she'd told Maria wasn't a lie. She was tired. She'd been sleeping like shit lately. So much on her mind, the only way to get to dreamland was by using, and the more she used, the more certain it became that Barry was going to find out she'd been skimming.

Fuck, now she'd started nodding off.

Jenni finished in the bathroom and grabbed a coffee carafe. At Ilya's table, she stood with a hip cocked. She didn't pour him a cup, even when he shoved the plain, thick white mug toward her.

"What are you doing here?" Her demand was crisp. Cool. Every word enunciated, since she had to struggle to make sure she wasn't slurring.

Ilya sat up straighter in the booth. "Getting something to eat, what does it look like?"

"Are you stalking me?" The words hissed out of her.

He started to laugh until he saw that she was serious. "What? No!"

"Look, this is where I work. You can't just show up here. I don't have time for this."

"Time for what? I'm not doing anything." It wasn't the truth, and they both knew it. Still, he tried to charm her with a smile.

A few months ago, it would have worked.

"You're going to get me in trouble." Jenni glanced over her shoulder with a frown. "Reggie doesn't like kids just hanging around. I can't give you anything for free, don't even ask."

"I don't need free anything. I came to get a burger and fries." Ilya pointed across the room. "There are tons of kids from school here, and he doesn't seem to mind *them* hanging out."

Jenni fixed him with a long, stern look that was designed to dig right into him. Whatever he thought he was up to, she wasn't having it. None of it. "I don't need you checking up on me, Ilya."

"I'm not even..." He cut himself off, tossed up his hands and shook his head. "Whatever. I'll just eat and go, okay? Sorry to cause you such *distress*."

For a second, she almost softened. They'd been friends so long. Too long for it to be like this between them. Too bad she couldn't figure out how else it ought to be. They wanted different things. They were different people.

Jenni took her coffee pot and returned to her section of the diner. She didn't look at him again, even though she could feel the burden of his stare all the way across the room. Ilya wanted her attention, and she couldn't give it to him, not even to fix whatever it was that had gone so spectacularly wrong between them.

She sent Maria over to him with his food. Jenni pretended not to notice when Lisa Morrow and her best friend Deana joined Ilya in the booth. Lisa was putting on a show, giggling and tossing her hair. Her laughter was loud and braying, determined to draw attention to the fact they were sitting together. It was so pathetic, so transparent, but with the drugs filtering through her now, Jenni could not bring herself to care. She'd heard a rumor that last year, Lisa had given Ilya a hand job at Benji Masterson's party. If Ilya wanted Lisa or Deana, he could have them both. If he was trying to make her jealous, he could just keep trying.

"Hey, Bob." Jenni managed a smile for one of her regulars. "Get you anything else?"

"You know, I b'lieve I'll take a little of that special

dessert you're so good about putting back for me." The trucker slid a wad of money across the table to her -- way more than it would take to pay for the eggs and pancakes he'd polished off.

Jenni tucked the cash into her apron pocket and counted out some change. She put it on the table, along with three pills he'd bought. Bob covered both the pills and the money with his hand and slid it toward him. It almost got away from him, one pill rolling toward the table's edge. He slapped his hand on it.

"Careful there, girl," he said to her, like it was her fault he'd been clumsy.

She nodded and moved away without a backward glance. She took the money and the check to the cash register and rang him out. Bob passed her on his way through the front door.

"You take care, you hear?" he said.

Jenni gave him another smile. "I always do."

She heard another swell of harsh and desperate feminine laughter but refused to turn to see what Lisa was laughing about. Jenni went into the kitchen instead. When she came out, Ilya was gone.

Good. She had the rest of her shift to finish, and she didn't want to get in trouble because Ilya was hanging around. Plus, she didn't want him to see her talking to Steve. So far, he hadn't shown up, and there was always the possibility that he wouldn't. Once again, he hadn't paged her when he said he would. That was what he did. Made her promises, didn't keep them, made her wonder if he'd ever promised them in the first place. Made her crazy.

For the rest of the night, she took and delivered orders, occasionally passing out the rest the drugs from her pocket in exchange for cash she went into the bathroom to count. She looked to the door every time it opened.

And then, an hour before she was due to leave, Steve finally came in. Her heart pounded at the sight of him. Excitement, but also a little anxiety. Maria sat him in Jenni's section, way in the back corner, but it took Jenni a few minutes before she could get over to him. She had to make sure her hands weren't trembling. That she could talk without stuttering.

"Hey," was all he said when she came up to offer him coffee and water.

It was how he greeted her every time. Same smirking smile. Same casual tone. If Ilya had spoken to her that way, like she barely mattered, Jenni would have hated him for it. But from *him, oh, him*, it was just how it should be.

"Am I giving you a ride home?"

She nodded. "Yes."

"Good."

She took his order. The usual. Steak and eggs, hash browns, biscuits with butter on the side. He was finishing up as her shift ended. She took his money without slipping him anything along with the change — he got better treatment than that. She'd have something special, something she held back, just for him, but would give it to him in the car when they parked. When he touched her. When he promised her he'd take her away with him.

"Jennilynn," Maria said as Jenni was clocking out. "Do you need a ride home? This weather is terrible."

"I have one, thanks."

Maria looked concerned. Her mouth, outlined in hot pink lipstick that had feathered into the wrinkles at the corners of her lips, pursed. "You sure? I can ask Reggie if he minds me cutting out a little early."

"I'm good," Jenni said and caught sight of Maria's stare. Uncomfortable and feeling caught out, Jenni frowned. "What?"

"He's too old for you," Maria said in a low voice. "And he's...well, there's been talk."

Jenni took a step back. Her heart pounded again, for different reasons this time. For all the care they'd taken, Maria must still have seen something in the way they spoke to each other. Maria was a nosy old bitch, but Jenni stopped herself from saying so.

"What kind of talk?" She expected Maria to say that people had been gossiping about her, and Jenni was ready to tell the older woman where those people could shove their tale-telling.

"He used to hit his wife," Maria said.

Jenni's mouth snapped shut so hard her teeth clipped the tip of her tongue. It should have hurt a lot more than it did. It would later. For now, she tasted a hint of blood.

"What?" It was all she could manage to say.

"He hit his wife," Maria repeated.

"His...wife." Steve didn't have a wife. He sometimes spoke with a twisted mouth and scorn of "the baby mama," but never mentioned a wife.

Maria nodded. "He used to be married to my cousin's hairdresser. She was always showing up to work with black eyes, busted lips. Said she was clumsy, but we all knew the truth."

"How long ago was that?"

Maria hesitated. "I don't know. I guess it's been some time, now."

"People change," Jenni said, although she knew that wasn't true.

"I'm just telling you," Maria said.

"He's a customer," Jenni told her.

Maria's brow furrowed. "Jennilynn..."

"I mean, he's *just* a customer." The lie came out in a steady voice, and Jenni made sure to stare directly into

Maria's eyes. She sounded convincing. "I'm not sure why you need to tell me this. I serve him breakfast, and he tips really well. What do you think is going on, exactly? I mean, do you think I'm sleeping with him?"

It was a trick she'd learned when dealing with her parents. If you acted like whatever it was that they were trying to get you to admit was totally out of line, they always backed down. It worked on Maria, too. The other waitress blinked rapidly and shook her head.

"No, of course not, I mean, that's just...no, hon, I'm sorry."

Jenni put a tremble in her voice. "I can't believe you'd think that about me."

"No, no. Of course I don't. It's just that I don't want you to get caught up in something you don't want to be in. That's all. You're a young and pretty girl. Men can be pigs. That's all, hon. I'm sorry."

"I have to go," Jenni said.

She went out through the kitchen door, untying her apron and balling it into her fist. A soft drizzle was falling, and Jenni tipped her face up toward it as she gulped in a few gasping breaths. She wanted to laugh at how Maria had backpedaled, but she was afraid if she let so much as a single chuckle escape her she would end up sobbing, instead.

He hit his wife. She couldn't even be shocked. Steve was rough with her, yeah, but in the way Jenni had learned she liked. Maybe the ex had liked it, too. Jenni swallowed a mouthful of mist, hoping to wash away the bitterness of her disappointment. Okay, so she wasn't the first. Why should that matter? She didn't love him, Jenni knew that. She was a little obsessed with him, sure. She liked fucking him, yes. She'd thought about them being together in the future, of course she had, because that's what he told her he wanted. Who knew, he might. Maybe he was in the market for a new wife, another future ex. Well, she wouldn't ever know unless she asked him, would she?

"Jenni."

She twisted, surprised at the sound of Ilya's familiar voice. Shame and guilt flooded her, along with a heady rush of delight that quickly became fear. He'd waited for her, and she couldn't risk letting him see her with Steve. Bad enough Maria had noticed something. Ilya could never know.

"What the hell are you doing here?" she demanded.

"I thought you might need a ride home." He moved closer.

"I have a ride home! Go away, Ilya! You need to go away, right now!" Incredibly, she shoved him hard enough to make him skid on the parking lot gravel. "Get out of here. I don't want you here! What is wrong with you?"

"I love you, that's what's wrong with me!" His shout was hoarse. His voice, cracked. He sounded like he might cry.

Oh, no. Not this. Not here, not now. Steve was waiting for her, and if she didn't want Ilya to see him, she also didn't want *him* to see Ilya.

Jenni pushed him again, harder this time. "I don't care, you can't be here. I don't want you here, okay? Just go."

"What did I do wrong?" Ilya cried, refusing to go. "Just tell me that."

She shook her head, unable to tell him that it was too late. Now, not the right time. He'd shouted out his love, sounding desperate and hungry, but he always did. That didn't make it love. Didn't make it real.

"You didn't...nothing...it's just that I don't need you here. Okay?"

"It's not okay!"

"Leave me alone, Ilya!"

"Fine. If that's what you want. Fine. Fuck you, Jenni." Ilya backed away, turning from her. "Forget it."

She tried to call him back, but although her mouth opened and closed and her tongue pressed her teeth, nothing came out but a hiss of air. She walked around the corner of the diner. Out of sight. The rain was really coming down now, and it soaked her. She shivered.

He pulled up in his black muscle car, motor rumbling. Rolled down the window. "Get in."

She did.

Chapter 19
REBECCA

Then

The rattle of rain on the roof of Tristan's car sounded like pebbles being tossed onto metal. Rebecca had run to his car with her coat over her head, but was still damp by the time she slid into the passenger seat. He had the heat blowing, but she was still chilled enough for her teeth to chatter as he put the car in gear without even greeting her.

They drove in silence for a minute before he said, "I thought maybe you were going to blow me off."

"My parents wanted me to stay in tonight because of the weather. I had to tell them I was going to study at a friend's house. Big test, you know?"

He laughed and glanced at her. "And what did you tell your boyfriend?"

"Same thing." Rebecca studied his profile, his eyes set back on the wet road in front of them. "Where are we going?"

"Someplace private. Don't worry. Nobody will see us."

On the Night She Died

She could have said she wasn't worried, but both of them would know the lie the second it left her lips. Since the night of the party, they'd never been together in public, never where anyone could see them. They weren't *dating*.

What were they doing, then?

She and Tristan had never spoken of the night in her room when he'd cried about his neighbor, but since that night, something had changed between them. If their mutual game had the single unspoken rule that they kept this all a secret, another had been added, and it was that they were no longer simply friends who fooled around. Whatever more had grown between them had no name, but it was there.

He'd stopped sneaking into her room after that night. Rebecca hadn't known it at the time when she'd woken to find him gone, but the housekeeper had seen him going out of her window when she was on her way in to work in the morning. Marisol hadn't told Rebecca's parents, but she swore she would if it happened again. So now, instead, they spent hours on the phone late at night when the house when her parents had gone to bed and the house was quiet. She'd never spent that much time talking to Richie. She and Richie had never had that much to say.

With Tristan, on the other hand, Rebecca always had too much to say. They argued a lot, about stupid things like favorite music and books and movies. About not-stupid things like religion, politics, the environment. He was a bad boy from the poor side of town with big ideas about how the world should work, especially for those without the money and privilege Rebecca had grown up enjoying. Their late night conversations often led to one or both of them threatening to hang up, to never speak to the other again, but somehow they always managed to end the phone call with the same whispered words.

"I'll talk to you again."

Tristan had been the first to say it, but now they both used it as a sort of shorthand for the rest of the words neither one of them could bring themselves to say aloud.

In person, they never argued. Sometimes, they barely spoke at all. When they met up, it seemed as though the secrets they were keeping from the world kept them silent with each other, too. In the back seat of his car, they kissed and touched, their conversation made up of soft sighs and groans and the occasionally muttered plea.

Rebecca had never known it could be like this. "It" being a relationship with a boy, and not only the physical part. Even though the great divide between their in-person and telephone time was enough to feel almost as though she was with two different people, she could never really allow herself even to pretend that everything she was doing centered on Tristan Weatherfield. The time on the phone was a friendship, a good, strong one that she valued. The time spent doing the other business was secrets and lies and betrayal. It would have been easier if she could partition it, but she couldn't.

This was not supposed to be love, but that's what it had begun to feel like.

A lightness when she thought of him. An overwhelming giddiness when it was almost time for him to call. An aching burn in her chest when she imagined graduation, the end of school, a brief summer and then she'd be off to college while Tristan did whatever it was he was going to do. They never talked about it. Whatever future lay ahead for both of them, the unspoken understanding was that it didn't involve each other.

Maybe he wanted his future to contain Allie Harrison, though. Rebecca had seen the two of them in school. Some sort of embrace. Not a kiss, but did that matter?

They could be friends in public. They could be more than that in public, if they wanted to, in a way that didn't feel possible for Rebecca and Tristan together.

Rebecca leaned forward to turn on the radio. The song, along with the steady beat of the wipers and the pattern of rain on the roof all went together so that she was humming along under her breath. Tristan glanced at her again, this time with a smile. Self-conscious about her singing, she stopped.

"Don't," he said. "I like it when you sing. It makes me think you're happy."

"I *am* happy." The impulse to admit it, say it out loud, surprised her, but she wasn't sorry she'd said it.

When he pulled up in front of a small duplex and killed the engine, Rebecca leaned forward to look through the windshield. Beneath the slash of rain on the glass, everything outside seemed to be moving. Unsettled, she sat back and looked at him.

"Your house?"

"Yeah. Is that okay? It's nasty out tonight. I just thought we could watch a movie or something. Hang out," Tristan added.

Rebecca nodded after a moment. "Sure. That's okay. Are your parents home?"

"My mom doesn't live with us anymore. I'm not sure where my dad is, but I figure he's on a job. He's a truck driver," Tristan told her. "He's usually gone for a week or so at a time, depending."

The idea of parents not being around all the time was intoxicating and unnerving. Rebecca's parents travelled once a year on vacation without her, but her grandparents always came to stay while they were gone. "That must be hard."

"No. It's better when he's not around. I mean, he's kind of hard to live with."

She twisted in the seat to look at him. In all their conversations, they hardly ever talked about Tristan's family life. Well, they hardly ever spoke about hers, either. They didn't have to talk about their lives to know how different they were.

"Tristan," she said, but stopped herself.

He waited, then smiled. He reached to tug one of her curls, watching it spring back up. "Rebecca."

She wanted, desperately, to ask him about Allie. If there was something going on. She didn't. What if he said yes? Could she be angry? Could she complain?

"Let's go inside," she said instead.

In Tristan's small and messy kitchen, she accepted a can of cola and popped the top. Sipping, she tried not to stare at the worn linoleum, the stack of dishes piled high in the drainer, the lack of a dishwasher. The yellow fridge. A food and water bowl sat on a mat by the back door. The kitchen smelled faintly of bleach overlaid with damp.

"The dog's been dead since last year. We just never seem to get around to getting another or getting rid of the bowls." Tristan looked embarrassed.

Rebecca shook her head, not sure what to say. He took her into the living room, where none of the furniture matched and all of it looked worn. The console television was ancient. He waved her toward the stairs instead of the couch.

"I have a DVD player upstairs. In my room."

She laughed. "Uh huh."

"It's true!" Tristan laughed, too.

Rolling her eyes, she followed him up the creaking stairs and into his room. It was cleaner than the other rooms had been. Same kind of worn furniture, but everything was tidy and organized. He had a small television on a stand with a DVD player and a collection of DVDs in a tall rack, along with a VCR and the accompanying tapes.

"I have a pretty big collection. Pick whatever you want."

Rebecca studied the movies, pulling out a plastic case that had once belonged to the local video store. She ran her fingers over the price sticker. "I didn't know they sold off their old movies. My parents usually just buy them. They don't even have a membership there."

"They're cheaper when you buy them used," Tristan said.

It wasn't the first time there'd been a glaring difference in the way they each looked at the world, but it was the first time it embarrassed her. She put the movie back. Tristan reached around her to pluck a different one from the rack, some kind of gun-chase comedy.

"How about this one?" He turned his face to look at her.

They stood so close she could count his eyelashes and see the faint spray of freckles across his nose. He'd pushed his thick sandy hair, wet from rain, off his forehead. She wanted him to kiss her.

He did.

It was so good, this thing with Tristan. All of it, except the parts where she couldn't tell anyone. The parts where she knew her parents would not approve. Where Richie would be hurt. Where her friends would all talk behind their hands about her. How she had to worry if there were other girls, or worse, just one other. How nobody could possibly understand this.

Tristan put the movie into the player, and they settled on the bed. He plumped the pillows so they could get comfy while watching. She leaned against his shoulder, their fingers linked companionably at their sides between them.

The movie played. Squealing tires. Shooting guns. Eventually, Rebecca pushed up on her elbow to offer her mouth to Tristan, who kissed her at once. Slow, sweet, lingering kisses that kindled a fire inside her that soon threatened to consume them both.

They'd fooled around a lot but had never gone this far. This wasn't the back seat of a car or the back row of a bargain movie theater just outside town or a sleeping bag in a field at the end of a dead end street. Tristan's bed had more than enough room for both of them to wriggle and roll.

Naked, he moved on top of her. Positioned himself. Kissed her. She kissed him back. Her arms went around him, pulling him down.

"Are you sure?" Tristan murmured into her ear.

Her body tensed, relaxed, every muscle answering for her. Still, she found her voice. "Yes. I'm sure. I want this. I want you."

It was supposed to hurt, but didn't. It was supposed to be good for him, and not for her, but it was. It was supposed to be a lot of things, but it was *not* supposed to be love.

"I love you," Tristan said. Then again. "Oh, God. I love you, Rebecca."

The words were there, fighting in her mouth to get free, but she was too consumed with the sudden, overwhelming pleasure rocking through her. She couldn't speak at all. Could only gasp and dig her nails into his back.

He said he loved her, and she drew blood.

Tristan was still on top of her when the first shouts rose outside his room. Something slammed into the hallway wall hard enough to rattle the cork board hung next to his bedroom door. Again, another slam, another shout. The crack of flesh on flesh.

It took Rebecca too long to figure out what was happening. Tristan was still on top of her when the door flew open so violently that it hit the wall. He pulled the covers up to shield her, but as he moved, she got a clear view of who was bursting through the door.

Jennilynn Harrison, blond hair tumbling over her shoulders, stumbled backward as the man in front of her pushed her without letting her move freely by keep his hand on her throat. She had her hands on his, but wasn't fighting him. He shook her in his grip, while his other hand drew back and slapped her across the face. Her entire body turned from the blow. Blood spattered from her split lip.

"Jesus Christ, Dad, get out!" Tristan shouted.

The older man, who bore little resemblance to Tristan, turned his bleary gaze on him. "The fuck are you doing here?"

"The fuck are *you* doing?" As he'd done the night of the party, Tristan tried to use his body to keep Rebecca out of sight, but it didn't work this time.

Jenni, clearly drunker even than her companion, staggered. Her gaze focused on Rebecca. "Holy shit.

"You're bleeding. Christ." Tristan tugged off the comforter to wrap around him, leaving Rebecca beneath the sheet, and grabbed a handful of tissues from the desk. He shoved them into the blond girl's hand. "Clean yourself up."

"Can't, can't," she said and threw the tissues all over the floor. She waved an unsteady hand toward Tristan's dad. "Has to look real or else they won't believe it."

"It looks real all right," Tristan said.

His father grabbed Jenni by the elbow and yanked her

through the door and into the hallway. "C'mon, you dumb bitch."

He didn't slam the door behind them, so Rebecca had no trouble watching as the older man kissed Jenni. What a mess. Both of them came away from it smeared with blood. Rebecca's stomach turned.

Just before they moved out of sight, Jenni looked over her shoulder at Rebecca. She was laughing, even with the blood dripping steadily from her lip and a pattern of dark bruises beginning to show on her neck. Her grin didn't read to her eyes. They looked blank, absent. Jenni looked like a ghost that had started haunting itself.

Tristan sat heavily on the edge of the bed. "God. Shit. I'm sorry, Rebecca. That was crazy."

"Did you know they were…umm…." She sat up to put her lips on his shoulder.

"No. I mean. God. Gross." He shuddered and turned his face to hers. "What the fuck, right? Jenni and my fucking *dad?*"

Rebecca shuddered at the thought of it, then again with regret how so special a night was now going to forever be tainted by what had just happened. "Will you tell your mother?"

He shook his head. "I told you. She doesn't live here, anymore."

"They're divorced."

"They didn't have to get divorced. They weren't married."

So that rumor had been true. Rebecca didn't know what to say. She let her forehead rest in the place her lips had kissed. Tristan breathed with a shiver. His skin goosepimpled.

"That was so fucked up," he whispered.

Chapter 20
JENNI

Then

This was what they were going to do.

Jenni would meet up with Barry tonight. She'd make him give her the pills, all of them. She wouldn't give him the money for them. She'd keep both.

"I'll just, you know." She said this to Steve with a wave of her hand, not finishing or planning to until he gave her a look of bland ignorance. "Seduce him."

"I don't fucking like that," he said, like he had any say in what she did.

Jenni rolled her eyes. "I won't really do anything with him. I'll just make him think I will. He's just gross enough he'll go for it."

"Needs more." Steve drew on his cigarette, making the cherry tip glow. "Gotta make sure he doesn't try to come after you for any of it. Or me. You need to make it so you can threaten to go to the cops. Black eye, split lip. That sort of thing. Tell him you'll tell the cops he did it."

"He won't hit me," Jenni said.

Steve snorted soft, derive laughter. "He doesn't have to."

Shit. Jenni startled awake. She'd nodded off in the front seat of Steve's car. She sat up straight with a groan at the stiffness in her joints and neck. Bruises. The rough twist of tissue tugged her nostril as she pulled it out.

"Don't get blood on my seats."

"Is that all you care about?" She twisted to look at him, barely able to focus.

Steve took his eyes off the road. The car swerved. Jenni screamed.

"Just shut up and let me drive," he said. "We're almost there."

Chapter 21
REBECCA

Now

So many plans to make, and Rebecca's mother didn't seem capable of making any of them. Dad had done most everything for Mom forever, or he'd hired people to do it for her. Now, she was lost.

"We can call a caterer," Rebecca said now, trying to be patient because God knew, all of this was hard enough without her losing her temper at her mother's helplessness. "Or order in food from someplace. I mean, I know we're in Quarrytown, but someplace has to deliver. Doesn't it?"

Jews, by tradition, were buried within as short a timeframe as possible. Her father had gone into the ground two days ago, but so far, her mother hadn't been able to organize the shiva. The seven-day period of mourning would happen at their house. People were supposed to *bring* food, Rebecca thought, but to be honest, she wasn't sure. Wouldn't it be better to have some, in case? Growing up, they'd never been very observant, and in the years since leaving home, she'd definitely never become more so.

"Is someone calling people or letting them know?" Rebecca asked now, gently, trying hard not to let her mother hear the frustration in her voice.

"Lorna is doing it."

Rebecca's ex-mother-in-law. She hadn't spoken to the woman in a decade, much to what Rebecca always assumed was their mutual relief. She sighed internally now. She could call Richie, see what was going on. That would mean she had to speak to him, but hell. Maybe he'd heard from Grant, who was still not answering her texts.

"We have to invite everyone he knew," her mother said now. "They'll all want to come."

Rebecca bit the inside of her cheek. "Daddy knew everyone, Mom."

"They'll *all* come to honor his memory." Her mother sniffled into her hankie.

What would it have been like, Rebecca wondered, to love Richie that much? To love anyone that much, other than herself? She loved her son beyond anything she'd ever dreamed could be possible, and she'd cocked that up in a way that seemed irreparable. She couldn't even begin to imagine giving her heart to a romantic partner so deeply that losing him would leave her devastated. The question was, did that make her envy her mother, or was she happy she would never have to suffer the way Mom was?

"Is it like a wake, or what?" Rebecca wracked her brain to remember anything she could about sitting shiva, finally pulling out her phone to search for information.

"We have to cover the mirrors. Tear our sleeves. We'll wear black ribbons."

Rebecca nodded. "Sure, Mom. Whatever you want."

"I'm going to have a nap. I'm so tired, Becky-boo."

Not even the hated nickname was going to make her

On the Night She Died

lose it with her mom. "That sounds like a good idea. You go, I'll figure this out."

With her mother resting, Rebecca thought about calling Lorna. Frankly, she didn't have the emotional wherewithal at the moment to face the woman who'd once referred to Rebecca as "that tart." Right now, Rebecca didn't have the strength for mourning her father, not for comforting her mother. Not for any of this.

It would be so easy to call for a car to take her to the airport. She could be somewhere else within a few hours. Anywhere else. Far away from Quarrytown, the place she'd run from and had never intended to come back to again.

At the very least, she needed to get out of the house right now and find a few bottles of wine and maybe a pack of cigarettes. She'd never taken up smoking as a habit and could take it or leave it, most of the time. Right now was more like a "take it" kind of night.

How weird to be behind the wheel of her dad's car. He'd only allowed her to drive it a handful of times, never without him beside her, coaching and guiding. The engine revved as she eased it down the driveway. The rural highway was a good place to open it up, and she hit eighty before having to slow down. It was a left-lane ride, as her dad had always been fond of saying, and again, Rebecca considered simply driving on. Through town and beyond. Take the car, she thought, and go, just…go.

Of course she wasn't going to do that. She certainly had been a disappointment to her parents, but she wasn't a terrible person. Mom needed her, and even though Rebecca didn't *want* to be here to participate in some ancient Jewish mourning ritual, she *was* here, and she was going to do whatever she could to help her mother.

The liquor store was in the same strip mall it had always been. No more familiar anchor stores, they'd all gone out of business, but most everything else looked the same. Inside, Rebecca tried to fool herself into thinking she could get away without a basket, but ended up grabbing a cart. She was going to stock up.

She had two bottles of a red blend in her hands when she turned and nearly dropped them both. The woman standing next to the cart had been trying to move past her, and she startled, too. Rebecca laughed self-consciously and set her bottles in the cart.

"Rebecca?" The woman asked. "Um, hi, it's me, Alicia. Harrison?"

"Oh. Wow. Allie! Alicia," Rebecca amended, since maybe the other woman had grown out of the nickname. "Hi. How are you?"

"I'm fine. I heard about your father. I'm sorry. Morry was a good guy."

Rebecca's throat closed. "You knew my dad?"

"Yeah. I mean…everyone knew him." Allie looked into the cart, but if she was judging the amount of wine in it, she didn't show it.

"We'll be having a shiva. Sitting shiva. A thing," Rebecca said quickly. "It's a Jewish thing that my mother wants."

Alicia gave her a small smile. "I know what it is. Sure. My grandmother-in-law passed not too long ago, and they sat shiva for her."

"You did? Here?" Rebecca paused. She'd heard that Alicia had married and then divorced Ilya Stern, but were the Sterns Jewish? In a town with a very small Jewish population, you'd have thought she would have known.

"Yeah."

"Can you help me figure out how to plan it?"

Alicia looked surprised. "Sure. I guess. I mean, if you need someone."

"I don't know anything about it. Mom said my ex-mother-in-law is helping organize it, but unless she's changed a lot, whatever that woman tries to plan is going to be a shitshow. Sorry. A clusterfuck. Sorry."

Alicia laughed. "Don't be sorry. Sure. I can help you figure out what to do. I don't know that much about it, but if you need help I'm happy to do what I can."

"Thank you," Rebecca said sincerely. "I'm trying to be the good daughter and figure out what would be appropriate. Do you have a few minutes? We can run next door. I'll buy you a coffee? Just let me pay for this."

In the small café next door they ordered coffees and took them to a small table by the front window. Alicia laid out what she knew about setting up shiva, and offered the name of the local rabbi. Rebecca didn't recognize her name, or the name of the synagogue.

"So much has changed around here," she said.

Alicia nodded. "Yep. You haven't been back in a long time."

"No. I wouldn't have come back at all, if not for my dad."

"I'm sorry. It's hard to lose someone. When Jennilynn died, it seemed like it would take forever to get over the loss. To be honest, I'm not sure I ever did. I know my parents haven't done a great job. And Ilya…" Alicia shrugged, looking embarrassed. "Sorry, I didn't mean to hijack your grief."

"It's fine. I didn't take it that way." Rebecca sipped coffee. "I'm sorry about your sister, too. It must have been harder for you all. She was so young, and it was so unexpected. My dad had been sick on and off for a long time."

"I don't know if that makes it any better. Losing someone you love is always hard, no matter what." Alicia gave Rebecca a small, sad smile.

Rebecca glanced at her watch. "I should get back to my mom. I left her napping. If she wakes up and I'm gone, she might worry."

"Sure, of course. Thanks for the coffee. If I can help you with anything else, let me know."

They both stood.

Rebecca hesitated, thinking of the long ago night when she and Tristan had been in his room and Jennilynn had barged in with his dad. It hadn't been much longer after that before the girl had been found dead. Neither she nor Tristan had come forward with that information back then. Steve Weatherfield had skipped town. She and Tristan had…well. They'd ended things, and not on a good note. Rebecca had gotten pregnant. Married. She'd left town. She had no idea where Tristan might have gone, or if he were still around.

Back at her parents' house, she checked on her mother. Still sleeping. With a bottle of wine and a crystal wine glass, Rebecca went into her childhood bedroom and opened up her laptop. It took only a few seconds to log in to her Connex account. She wasn't active on there, preferring photo-based social media because it was easier to keep track of her pictures that way.

She found Tristan's profile with only another minute or so of searching. She scanned it. According to the information, he was married, and he still lived in Quarrytown.

Married, she thought. Well. Damn.

Then she closed her laptop and went about the very serious business of drinking that wine.

Chapter 22
JENNI

On the Night She Died

Jenni's skin crawled at Barry's touch. She'd known it, *known* he was a fucking perverted creepo who'd be down to get it on with her. Even when she showed up with the bloody mouth and the start of the black eye, all she had to do was crooked her finger, and he was ready to go.

"What the hell do you mean, give you the pills? *You* give me the cash," Barry demanded when they'd finished what had passed for their sordid coupling. He hadn't even been able to get hard. She should be glad he only slobbered all over her. "That's how this works."

"Nope. How this worksh...works," she restated to be more clear, "is that you're going to give me the pills and the money. I'm getting out of here. I need product, and I need cash."

Barry shook his head. "No fucking way."

They hadn't met at the house, because Galina was home from work. She was the one who stole the pills from the hospital, but she'd always insisted she never wanted to know anything about what happened to them after that. Barry and Jenni had met in the old equipment shed instead. Cold rain slanted through the holes in the roof, and Jenni shook with the chill. Her chattering teeth annoyed her, and she clenched her jaw to make them stop.

"What happened to your face?"

"You asked me that already." She touched her lip. She knew it should hurt, but she'd taken a couple of pills and wasn't feeling much of anything.

"You didn't answer me." Barry pulled his coat up around his neck. "Jesus, Jennilynn. You're a mess. What the hell is going on with you? Who did this? Dillon?"

"Not him. You." She tried to laugh, but it came out mushy and unformed. She jabbed a finger at him. "You did this to me. Or that's what I'm going to tell everyone unless you give me those pills. Oh, *and* the money."

"Not happening." Barry shook his head.

Jenni took a step toward him, but the ground was uneven and her balance no good. She fell forward, smacking her knee against a rotting office chair and hitting her head on the shed's wall for good measure. She fought off Barry's hands when he tried to help her up.

"I'll tell them you hit me! And raped me! And whatever else I want!" That's what she thought she shouted, but the words stuttered and wouldn't come out right. She laughed again, the sound a mumbled jumble, a slurring mutter. It's really all she could manage. "I'll tell Galina you fucked me."

"Jesus, we barely...we didn't even." Barry recoiled.

"She'll believe me. Doesn't matter if the cops don't, but they would too."

Barry shook his head. "You've clearly been fucking someone else."

"I'll tell them, ,and show them, and what the hell, I'll tell them about the pills, too. Then you'll be the one who gets fucked." This seemed hilarious to her. Barry didn't seem to agree.

"Jesus, fuck. Don't. Please," he said.

Pathetic piece of shit. Jenni wove, standing still but unsteady. She hated him. If not for him, she'd never have done any of this. She would never have gone with Steve.

"Give me the pills! And the money!" She shouted, her voice hoarse and breaking.

"Fuck," Barry cried. "What the fuck am I supposed to tell Galina about the money? She counts it, you know!"

"You think I give one tiny little damn what you tell your *wife*?" She sneered the word.

"I don't have any of it. You think I carry all of that around with me all the time?"

He was lying, she thought. "Why'd you meet me here, then?"

"To *get* my money from you, you stupid little bitch."

Jenni spat a fresh gobbet of blood onto the ground. "Why is that men always call us stupid bitches when they don't get their own way?"

Barry didn't answer her on that. He pushed past her, pausing in the shed's rotten doorway. "Just…get some help. If you tell me who he is, I'll make him stop hurting you."

She didn't answer him. Barry left. He didn't really want to help her, Jenni thought. Nobody ever did.

Outside, she fought through the chill rain and the trees that slapped her in the face and bruised her even more. She stumbled from the edge of the treeline and made it to the passenger side of Steve's car, parked in the dead end of the cul-de-sac. Ballsy of him. If anyone in her house or the Sterns' across the street looked outside, they could possibly see it, even though the black car blended into the night.

They'd wonder who was parked there. They might even come out to check, or call the police.

The door didn't open. Locked. Motherfucker. She went around to the driver's side. He rolled down the window.

"You get the stuff?"

"He didn't have it!" she said, trying to get his door open.

Steve pushed her hand away from the handle and then pushed her back with a rough shove to her chest. She stumbled and went onto her ass. Startled more than hurt, since she was still feeling hardly any pain, Jenni got to her feet.

"I'm out of here," he told her. "Go home, little girl."

"Wait. I thought we were leaving town. Together?"

Steve spit into the rain. "Nah. Not unless you can get me the stash and the cash, bitch."

Again with the *bitch*. She was fed-fucking-up with this bullshit, but when she tried to tell him so, all she could manage was a garbled mutter. Jenni tried to stand up straight but couldn't quite manage. Another rush of rain pounded down, soaking her.

Steve revved the engine and pulled the car around the cul-de-sac's curve so fast she had to jump out of the way. She fell on her ass again, this time in the muddy grass on the other side of the curb. She stayed there, trying to shout a few curses at him but unable to get her mouth to work right.

Fuck Steve. Fuck Barry and Galina, and Ilya Stern, fuck everyone in this town. Jenni staggered through the grass to the woods beyond. The trail was invisible in the dark and rain, but her feet found the way by long years of habit, not sight.

She didn't think about where she was going, or why. She thought only of the slow rise of pain in all the places she'd allowed Steve to hurt her. Of the pain beneath all the bruises and cuts that none of Barry's pills could numb. She thought of plans and fear and grief.

She thought of love, and the lack of it.

The rock outcropping where they put their towels in the summer was slick with wet and dark as the night surrounding it. Jenni went to her hands and knees on the rough surface. Her chin hit the rock. She pushed up on her hands, crawling to the edge.

Water below.

Water from the sky above.

Water, all around.

She got to her feet and put her toes to the rock's rim. Arms out. Face tipped to the sky, mouth open so it could fill with rain. She stayed like that forever, an eternity. For the rest of her life.

One step forward was all it took. She hit the rocks. Then the water.

There was no more pain.

The Quarry Street Series...

This sexy romantic drama from *New York Times* and *USA Today* bestselling author Megan Hart begins with the tangled lives—and loves—of childhood friends in All the Lies We Tell...

Everyone knew Alicia Harrison's marriage to Ilya Stern wouldn't last. They'd grown up on a remote stretch of Quarry Street, where there were two houses, two sets of siblings, and eventually, a tangled mess of betrayal, longing, and loss. Tragedy catapulted Allie and Ilya together, but divorce—even as neighbors—has been relatively uncomplicated.

Then Ilya's brother, Nikolai, comes home for their grandmother's last days. He's the guy who teased and fought with Allie, infuriated her, then fled town without a good-bye. Now Niko makes her feel something else entirely —a rush of connection and pure desire that she's been trying to quench since one secret kiss years ago. Niko's not sticking around. She's not going to leave. And after all that's happened between their families, this can't be anything more than brief pleasure and a bad idea.

But the lies we tell ourselves can't compete with the truths our hearts refuse to let go…

The story continues in All the Secrets We Keep…In the riveting conclusion to Megan Hart's passionate new family drama, the secrets they keep are no match for the truths their hearts will never let go.

Still stuck in his small Central Pennsylvania hometown, Ilya Stern is used to feeling like a disappointment. After his high school girlfriend, Jennilynn, drowned, he married her sister, Alicia, only to divorce a decade later. The business they started together is threatened by a luxury development—and Alicia has already sold her stake. Now that Babulya, Ilya's gentle Russian grandmother, has died, there's no one left who believes in him. Or so he thinks.

Theresa Malone was Ilya's stepsister for only a year, until his mother threw her pill-popping father out of the house in the middle of the night, forcing teenage Theresa to follow. Now she's returned for Babulya's funeral—and to facilitate the quarry-development deal. As she tries to convince Ilya to sell, she realizes her feelings for him have ignited—from sisterly into something more.

Working together closely, Ilya and Theresa struggle to

define their intense attraction. When the details of Jenni-lynn's death surface, will Ilya and Theresa's deep connection keep their hope for the future afloat—or submerge them once and forever in their tragic past?

All the Lies We Tell
All the Secrets We Keep

The Quarry Street Series
continues...

All the Truths We Reveal

Coming soon!

Tristan Weatherfield grew up a cliché. Wrong side of the tracks, poor family, trouble with the law. He was the quintessential bad boy with a thing for the golden good girl. Rebecca Segal, smart, poised, heir to the fortune of one of Quarrytown's most prominent families.

The Quarry Street Series continues...

Of course Tristan and Rebecca were wrong for each other.

Of course they fell in love.

Or lust, at least. Passion. Furtive and delicious and exciting and fraught with guilt.

The night they witnessed some of fellow student Jennilynn Harrison's final moments signaled the end of a relationship that had never been meant to last. Bonded forever by what they saw that night and the death of their classmate, Tristan and Rebecca nevertheless part ways and don't keep in touch.

Now, Rebecca's father has passed away and she's back in Quarrytown. Dealing with her ex-husband, her former high school boyfriend, her estranged son and her distraught, helpless mother, leaves Rebecca ready to flee this small town the first chance she gets...just the way she did so many years ago.

Yet when she and Tristan get back in touch, their former passion and friendship is undeniable. With even more secrets between them than either of them know and neither willing to be vulnerable, their past seems destined to haunt them forever worse than any ghost ever could.

Also by Megan Hart

All the Lies We Tell
All the Secrets We Keep
A Heart Full of Stars
Always You
Broken
Castle in the Sand
Clearwater
Crossing the Line
Deeper
Dirty
Don't Deny Me
Everything Changes
Every Part of You
Flying
Hold Me Close
Indecent Experiment
Lovely Wild
Naked
Out of the Dark
Passion Model
Precious and Fragile Things
Reawakened Passions
Ride with the Devil

Selfish is the Heart

Stranger

Stumble into Love

Switch

Tear You Apart

Tempted

The Darkest Embrace

The Favor

The Resurrected: Compendium

The Space Between Us

Vanilla

About the Author

I was born and then I lived awhile. Then I did some stuff and other things. Now, I mostly write books. Some of them use a lot of bad words, but most of the other words are okay.

I can't live without music, the internet, or the ocean, but I have kicked the Coke Zero habit. I can't stand the feeling of corduroy or velvet, and modern art leaves me cold. I write a little bit of everything from horror to romance, and I don't answer to the name "Meg."

Megan Hart is a USA Today, Publisher's Weekly and New York Times bestselling author who writes in many genres including mainstream fiction, erotic fiction, science fiction, romance, fantasy and horror. If you liked this book, please tell everyone you love to buy it. If you hated it, please tell everyone you hate to buy it.

Find me here!
www.meganhart.com
readinbed@gmail.com

Made in the USA
Monee, IL
16 March 2021